FORGOTTEN MEN

The Bayou Hauntings
Book Two

Bill Thompson

Published by
Ascendente Books
Dallas, Texas

Forgotten Men: The Bayou Hauntings, Book 2
Published by Ascendente Books
ISBN 978-09979129-8-2
Printed in the United States of America

Books by Bill Thompson

The Bayou Hauntings
CALLIE
FORGOTTEN MEN

Brian Sadler Archaeological Mystery Series
THE BETHLEHEM SCROLL
ANCIENT: A SEARCH FOR THE LOST CITY
OF THE MAYAS
THE STRANGEST THING
THE BONES IN THE PIT
ORDER OF SUCCESSION
THE BLACK CROSS
TEMPLE

Apocalyptic Fiction
THE OUTCASTS

The Crypt Trilogy
THE RELIC OF THE KING
THE CRYPT OF THE ANCIENTS
GHOST TRAIN

Middle Grade Fiction
THE LEGEND OF GUNNERS COVE

This book is dedicated to my readers who enjoyed Callie, the first in the Bayou Hauntings series, and asked for more.

That book was my initial venture into a new genre, and thanks to your comments, I knew what to write next!

I appreciate your interest in my books and your support.

CHAPTER ONE

Louisiana's "Most Haunted Building"
Destroyed in Spectacular Blaze

The six o'clock news was ending as the story about the inferno in a ghost town south of New Iberia broke. At eight, a reporter from Channel Nine in New Orleans interrupted network programming to report on the doomed four-story wooden structure.

In all the confusion, journalists missed two important clues that would have made the story really interesting. First, a Louisiana State Police lieutenant and three uniformed men already had perimeter security and a command post established by the time the news people arrived by helicopter. The cops were from Baton Rouge, a hundred miles away, and they'd apparently been there long before the fire started. If so, why had they come?

Second, only firefighters and lawmen were allowed around the sides and back of the massive old building. Sheriff's deputies kept everyone in the front "for safety reasons." Only the authorities knew that the real story here — and the answer to how the fire started — had played out in an old cemetery at the back of the property.

Fires always make exciting news, and the blaze consuming this cavernous two-hundred-year-old building was truly spectacular. As the sun set, flames soared from the windows on the upper floors, rotten wood crackled like a campfire, and firefighters pushed each other back as upper walls began to implode. Broadcasting from a place in the former prison's parking lot with the fire behind her, a journalist recounted the bizarre facts that had recently made this place newsworthy. Her producers created a spooky tale, playing the ghost angle that they hoped would captivate viewers.

Clouds of smoke swept around her now and then as she spoke into the microphone. "The historic main building at the long-abandoned Victory Institution for the Criminally Insane is enveloped in flames right now, and we're told that firefighters intend to let it burn itself out. This marks the end for a building that began life in 1820 as one of the grandest hotels in the South. Today, the Louisiana Society for the Paranormal calls it the most haunted building in Louisiana. The fire is in the main structure of the former institution, which people in the area nicknamed the Asylum. It sits on several acres along the Bayou Teche in rural Iberia Parish near Victory.

"Victory is a ghost town. Everyone left in the mid-1800s when the railroad bypassed it. The hotel closed, and one of the first for-profit prisons in America operated there from 1875 until 1907. The building has sat empty ever since — unless you believe the people at the Louisiana Society for the Paranormal, who say it isn't empty at all. They say the spirits of the damned — prisoners they call 'Forgotten Men'

— have never left this dismal prison. They're doomed to haunt the place forever unless tonight's fire somehow frees their souls."

Channel Nine's people scrambled to maintain the exclusivity they had gained by being on the scene first. While the newscaster talked on air, others were hard at work nearby, making sure their station would have something really special for its viewers down the line.

A few hours later when the ten o'clock newscast aired, the fire was the lead story, and there was a tantalizing announcement when it ended.

"We're preparing a special report on the famous hotel that became an infamous penitentiary. Next week we'll bring you a two-hour special called 'Victory and the House of Horrors.' Using archival material, we'll show you how the beautiful Hotel Iberia looked in the early 1800s and how it appeared as the most terrible prison in Louisiana history.

"You'll meet Landry Drake, the former deputy sheriff who linked a series of mysterious deaths at the Asylum and solved a thirty-year-old mystery. Using cellphone video he took himself, Drake will take our viewers inside the ancient cellblocks and reveal spine-chilling images that you may find hard to believe. Landry Drake knows something evil haunts the prison, because he was a prisoner here.

"Noted authorities on both sides of the issue — a ghost hunter and a skeptic — will debate the question of haunted buildings. After hearing their thoughts and seeing the video from inside this eerie, forbidding place, you can decide for yourself if you believe, as many do, that someone — or something — has haunted the Asylum for over a century."

CHAPTER TWO

For two hundred years before the night of the fire, the turrets on the corners of the building had pierced the dark sky like ghostly fingers grasping for a man's soul. Once — a long time ago, before the War tore apart the country — this had been the grandest hotel in the South, a showplace where gentlemen and ladies mixed with others of their kind, ignoring everything in the world but themselves, their desires and needs.

Those were the good days, the days before first the railroad and then the War changed everything. After that, the once opulent hotel morphed into something else — a dark, ominous place people whispered about.

It became the Asylum.

Victory, Louisiana, had been a ghost town for a very long time. These days, only two buildings still had four walls — the ones a rich man named Frank Connolly built out of bricks. Even in a decaying state, visitors could imagine how grand they must have been in the town's prime. One had the single word *bank* etched into a lintel above its entrance. The other was a far more imposing three-story structure. In stone along the top of the building were the words *Connolly Investments*. Everything else in Victory — the stores and businesses that had flanked ten blocks of the broad avenue — today lay in various stages of ruin. For most, only the foundations remained as silent reminders that Victory had once been a vibrant community.

Next to the Bayou Teche about a half mile from downtown stood another abandoned structure, a huge building that had been the area's grandest hotel. Erected in 1820, its four stories made it the tallest structure in Victory, and it was also the largest. It was still intact — the walls, floors and roof were still in place, although they were badly deteriorated from abandonment and neglect. Turrets on its corners gave it a Gothic appearance, and the empty windows stared out like black eyes onto grounds that had once been home to fancy gatherings and afternoon tea parties.

A large concrete sign stood at the entry gate. Its words revealed what a once-great hotel had become. *Victory Institution for the Criminally Insane.* Six simple words that described a place of horror.

The decaying structure had begun life as the Iberia Hotel, the brainchild of Frank Connolly, the town's mayor and the wealthiest man to ever live in this parish. It opened in July 1820, and according to historical documents, it had been an overnight success. People came from miles around to see and be seen in the vast lobby, stay in one of thirty-five professionally decorated guest rooms, and stroll the lavish grounds. Every few months, Connolly held a fancy ball with an orchestra brought in all the way from New Orleans. Sophisticated Southern belles spent hours with their handmaidens fretting over which gown to wear. When their chic horse-drawn surreys arrived at the hotel's entrance, valets assisted ladies and beaus resplendent in evening dress. Townspeople young and old gathered at the edge of the driveway to watch. The guests, aloof and detached, secretly loved the gasps, oohs and aahs from the less fortunate. Each lady prayed she would be the most elegant dame in the Grand Salon tonight.

For thirty years, the lavish hotel was the primary venue for socializing along Bayou Teche, but around 1850, Victory was dealt a losing hand.

Rail routes were being laid out. They spelled prosperity for the lucky communities chosen for a stop, and doom for those who were not. Municipal leaders in small parish towns like Jeanerette, Olivier, Charenton and Victory lobbied for a station, but in the end, New Iberia became the only train stop for the parish. People abandoned the small towns and moved close to the railroads, which meant jobs and a future. Iberia Parish was no different. Three of the losing towns in the contest suffered, shrank in population but survived. The fourth one died. That one was Victory.

Connolly was gone by then — he sold the hotel in 1838 and moved up north somewhere. Within twenty years, the town was deserted. Empty houses, stores and churches were surrendered to the elements. No one cared about them anymore. The once-grand hotel couldn't survive; when guests stopped coming, its owner shut it down in 1859. During the Civil War, it served as a Union barracks. If there had been anyone left in Victory, there would have been cries of outrage over Yankees staying in town. But Victory was dead. All that remained were shells of buildings and a memory of what once had been.

After the war, the governor decided to construct a very special kind of prison — one that wouldn't be popular no matter where it was built. Ideally, this facility needed to be remote, away from populated areas, and far from public view. And it would be privately owned so the state could deny responsibility if things went wrong. The nation's first for-profit prison — San Quentin — had opened in 1852, and things were going well there, so lawmakers in Baton Rouge thought it might work here too.

Businessmen began considering how to profit from the governor's idea. One consortium thought the ghost town of Victory was perfect because there were no citizens to protest. The owners bought the old hotel, greased the right palms up at the state capitol, and won a long-term contract to run a prison for the state of Louisiana.

The new facility would house Louisiana's most hopeless, dangerous men. It was a godsend for the state, and lawmakers gladly paid for renovations to convert the four-story hotel into a maximum-security penitentiary.

Contractors built a brick wall ten feet high around the property's perimeter, reinforced interior walls, and fitted windows with stout iron bars. The former hotel room doors were replaced with solid metal ones that had tiny viewing windows and a slot to pass food trays and chamber pots to prisoners, who would rarely leave their cells.

The Asylum opened in the summer of 1875, and by one measure — population — it was an immediate success. State prison officials used Victory as a dumping ground. All of its inmates had mental issues, and most were violent and aggressive. The prisoners weren't given medicine, so dangerous situations flared up every day, often ending with a body being hauled to its cemetery.

A prison creates commerce and wages. It wasn't long before the Asylum was the largest employer in the parish, and every dark whisper about how people were treated out there was answered with a shush and a wink. A prison was good for business, and people kept their mouths shut.

Originally, the prison board planned to house seventy inmates in the former hotel's thirty-five large bedrooms. Before the first week passed, it was clear that these men didn't acclimate well to cramped quarters and roommates. One prisoner died on opening day, and at the end of the first week, seven more were dead.

The state had spent a lot of money transforming the hotel into a prison, and all those deaths were bad publicity for their novel project. When the consortium requested more funding to build a new, high-security housing unit, the legislature said yes. Bad money after good, people would say later, as more and more prisoners were crammed in behind those walls. Soon there were a hundred inmates, then two hundred, then more.

Behind the four-story wooden building that had been the hotel, a long, low structure was built out of blocks. It resembled a horse barn, except that horse barns had something this hellhole for humans didn't — windows. Eighty tiny rooms held the incorrigibles and the insane, the only ventilation coming from doors at each end that could be opened during warm weather. Usually that didn't happen —

either the guards didn't care, or they kept the doors closed to punish the men who occupied the tiny cages. There was a guard station outside the building, one with plenty of windows and lots of sunshine pouring in. The theory was that Asylum guards shouldn't have to endure the same awful conditions as the prisoners. Guards stayed out there, playing cards and smoking cigarettes, while men died inside.

In this building men didn't die from fights, because they never had direct contact with others. These deaths were from food deprivation, torture and beatings by cruel guards, or from illnesses that went untreated until an inmate finally gained his release.

The atrocities that happened inside this ghastly place created a need for something else: a place to bury people nobody wanted — the unclaimed corpses of forgotten men. Prisoners stayed busy building pine boxes, and every few days guards stuffed in a body and nailed the top closed. Several hundred yards towards the back in a copse of trees, inmates dug graves. There were no tombstones remembering the dead — no stones or nameplates. All that marked the final resting places of the forgotten men were wooden crosses, one for each plot, stuck in the ground not to honor a man's life, but for the convenience of gravediggers. It was crowded in the cemetery, and they needed to know where to dig the next hole.

Although those crosses contained information, even in death the deceased received no dignity. The crosses didn't show a man's name; instead there was a prison number, a one-word description of his crime, and the date he had gained his release from this hell on earth. A human being, a man who was born and named by his parents — a man who had chosen the wrong path — would be memorialized as V28505, Murderer, 11/28/1903.

Legislators loved the place because it filled a need. Louisiana's most dangerous offenders weren't the state's problem anymore. But around the turn of the century, tales began to surface — unbelievable stories of atrocities at the Asylum. Once newspaper reporters in Baton Rouge and New Orleans got on the scent, lawmakers were forced to acknowledge the rumors of shocking barbarities.

Behind closed doors, a Senate committee grilled the warden. He was neither creative nor intelligent, and interrogators quickly peeled away the veneer and realized exactly what kind of place he was running. Appalled committee members were sworn to secrecy, but as usual in politics, the word got out. The lead story on the front page of the New Orleans *Times-Picayune* on January 19, 1907, carried a one-word headline in bold, black type.

TORTURE!

An outraged public learned about the atrocities at Victory's Asylum. Granted, these were society's dregs, but common decency required civil treatment of human beings. A few beatings here and there would have been one thing, but what the warden had disclosed about the prison was far more than any reasonable person could tolerate.

Elected officials couldn't hide the problem any longer. Subpoenas went out for the owners, who smoothly denied any knowledge about the prison's day-to-day operations. A grand jury met and heard testimony, and three men who had benefitted from the loathsome treatment of others — two owners and the warden — were each sentenced to a decade behind bars. Over the ensuing months, several of the particularly savage guards were jailed too. Putting a former guard in prison alongside the inmates he'd beaten half to death was a recipe for disaster, as many guards learned the hard way.

The prison at Victory didn't last much longer. Legislators got the message from their constituents and the press, and the state prison board voted to close the Asylum and move the inmates to Louisiana State Penitentiary in Angola.

On the day in 1907 when the last person walked out of the huge old administration building, there were three hundred wooden crosses sticking out of the ground in that godforsaken cemetery out back. Today they were scattered everywhere, making it impossible to know exactly where anyone was buried. Regardless, they were there. Three hundred rotting wooden boxes, each containing the body of a deeply disturbed, incredibly violent man, lay just beneath the loamy soil in the shade of tall oak trees.

Three hundred corpses waited.

For justice.

For revenge.

CHAPTER THREE

Victory, Louisiana
Twelve Years Ago

Sitting on the rotting front steps, Landry wished to God he hadn't taken the dare. Everything seemed to be working in tandem to scare the daylights out of this thirteen-year-old boy. The dark, ominous building seemed to reach to the low-hanging clouds. Rumbles of thunder growled in the distance. Ten feet across the porch was the front entrance. Its door had rotted away ages ago, and now there was a black, gaping hole that led somewhere frightening.

Landry could hear sounds from deep within the bowels of the old structure. Those murmurs and groans were just the wind, right? It had to be the wind. What else could it be? Now there was a scraping sound, and in between the thunderclaps, he thought he'd heard whispers. Despite the scary stories his brother had left him with before dropping him off, Landry assured himself that what he was hearing was normal. The noises were what you'd expect from inside a two-hundred-year-old building. It was the building making those noises, not the moans and whispers of inmates who had been brutally tortured until they died.

I'm not afraid. I'm not afraid.

If I keep repeating that, maybe I'll believe it.

As a storm approached, the wind whipped through the trees with a fury, and Landry zipped his jacket against the cold. He wished he'd brought his heavy coat, but the dare had come so fast there wasn't time to make plans. It would be warmer once he was inside — and inside was where he had to go anyway. His brother had taunted him, telling him he was too chicken to go in, because the Asylum was the most haunted building in the parish. To prove he wasn't a coward — and earn his cash reward — Landry had to go inside. He was determined to follow through because Larry Drake, his brother, had never been inside, and he was a seventeen-year-old macho football star.

I'll do it. I'm freezing out here anyway. There's nothing in there to be afraid of.

Seconds later, he had to move. It began to rain; there were big fat drops at first, then came a gullywasher of a storm. As powerful gusts of wind whipped across the veranda, Landry ran to the dark hole where a door had been, and stepped inside.

What would have been an unsettling place back in the day was frightening now. Eerie shadows engulfed a broad front room that was once a reception area. Landry saw a counter where people would have signed in. His brother said that when the place closed in 1907, everything inside had been left behind, but over the years vandals had destroyed everything. Now what had once been chairs and tables had been reduced to piles of wood.

Where once had been a steel-framed security door separating the public area from the prison, there was now a gaping hole. Long ago, someone had ripped out the door and frame and took them away to sell. A sign over the doorway dangled from one nail. "No Visitors Beyond This Point," it warned, although now there was nothing to keep trespassers from venturing through the doorway.

As his eyes became accustomed to the darkness, he became less scared and more interested in the cavernous structure. After all, it was just an old building — an insane asylum for killers, as Larry had called it in the tale he told his little brother. But now it was just an old, empty building.

"People died in the Asylum, hundreds of them," Larry had whispered in a spooky voice. "Their bodies are buried somewhere on the property. They may be long gone, but you can still hear their screams of anguish and the ghostly laughs of prison guards who enjoyed whipping and beating the inmates until they could take no more." Larry paused, saw fear in his brother's eyes, and created even more theatrics. "They'd chain the prisoners up, leaving them without food or water in their cells until they died a horrible death!" He paused for a moment, enjoying the effect his terrifying description was having on his little brother. "The shrieks of dying men could be heard all the way into town, and people who lived in Victory would shut their windows and doors, hoping not to have to hear more.

"Some of the guards lived in our town, right here in Jeanerette. They'd go to bars after work and tell stories of what happened there. Everyone locked up in the Asylum was a total psychopath, Landry. There were murderers, rapists, kidnappers, men who tortured just for fun, and some who cut their victims into pieces. They were sent to the Asylum, but their horrific acts didn't stop. They kept on killing because the guards were afraid to stop them. One night one of the inmates even ..." Larry paused.

As horrible as the story was, Landry found himself unable to resist temptation. "Even *what?*"

"One guy killed a guard and *ate* his flesh! Right there inside the cellblock. He cut him up and ate him!"

"Holy shit!" his little brother murmured, fear engulfing his mind and body. *Surely this story wasn't true!*

"You're bullshitting me, Larry! You're trying to scare me."

Then came the dare. "You don't believe me? Think you have the balls to spend even one hour inside that place? Grown men have tried, and they've come out with their hair turned totally white, babbling like a baby, and they were insane for the rest of their lives."

Bullshit. "Yeah, right."

"Okay. I dare you to spend an hour at the Asylum. Just one hour. I'll drop you off, and I'll come back to pick you up." Larry reached into the glove box and pulled out a marking pen. "You have to go in and write your name on the wall at least a hundred feet back. That's to prove you were there in case I want to go look at it."

"What do I get if I do it?"

"Fifty bucks."

Landry's eyes widened. That was a lot of money. Larry could afford it — he had a job at the Jeanerette Feed Store — but fifty dollars was a week's pay. That showed how confident he was that his brother wouldn't take the dare. But he didn't know how much Landry wanted that money. He had a paper route, but that didn't bring in anything close to what his older brother made. He'd been saving for a new bike, and that would put him over the top.

How hard can it be? Just one hour in an old building that used to be a prison. I have to go in there and write my name on the wall. Big deal. All that stuff Larry said about how some inmate was a cannibal had to be total bullshit, but regardless he was terrified to go in there alone.

And now that was where Landry stood.

Once he was inside, the creaks and groans sounded much louder. The wind sighed through the huge front room and down a drafty old hallway that ran somewhere toward the back. He thought he heard people talking. The words were too faint to understand, and he forced himself to quit thinking like that. There were no people and certainly no ghosts in here. All four stories — all those cells — were empty now, just like they had been for over a hundred years. Vagrants had been inside and rats too. There was plenty of evidence of that, but he was the only living thing in the Asylum now.

There's no one here but me. Just me.

He had to believe that or he'd never get through the next forty-nine minutes.

He forced himself to put one foot in front of the other, heading into the blackness where the door had been. He switched on his flashlight and saw a very long hallway with rooms on both sides. Cells, actually. There were no doors now — as he walked down the hall, he saw metal toilets in some, a ruined bed or chair in another.

Landry was on alert, but he missed something high above, up near the ceiling, where wispy, feathery, smoky threads curled about. Although there was no wind to move them, they drifted, meandering lazily downwards as Landry stood in the hall below.

About fifty feet in, he decided he'd gone far enough to write his name on the wall. He took out the marker and scrawled "Landry Drake" and the date. As he finished, he felt something — a light bump. Something had brushed along his back as he faced the wall.

He turned sharply, but there was nothing there.

Help me.

What was that? Was it the wind?

Help me. Now there were soft, quiet words, where before there had been whispers in the wind. It was Larry, trying to scare him. It had to be. *God, make it be him.*

"Larry?" he cried out, his voice breaking. "Stop doing that! This isn't funny!"

Nothing but the same creaks and groans from somewhere deep in the structure.

He glanced around, and for the first time he noticed a translucent thing floating in the air.

Help me, it seemed to say as it brushed his shoulder, and he fainted.

Landry didn't know how long he'd been lying on the dusty, trash-strewn floor. All he knew was he needed to get the hell out of there now. He got up, grabbed his light, and ran as fast as he could through the doorway and into the reception room. He flew past the entryway and across the porch, running frantically through the driving rainstorm until he saw headlights. He jumped into the front seat, and Larry yelled at him for getting everything wet.

"I don't care about your damned car! You were in there!" Landry screamed, fighting back tears. "You tried to scare me!"

"Not me, little brother. I was at the ShopRite a mile away. Here's my Coke to prove it."

As they drove away, Larry asked if Landry wrote his name on the wall.

"Yes," he muttered. "I did it, and you owe me fifty bucks."

"Would you spend another hour in there for a hundred?"

He shook his head. He wouldn't go in there again for anything in the world. That was the most scared that Landry Drake had ever been in his entire life, and it would be twelve years before he visited the Asylum again.

CHAPTER FOUR

New Iberia, Louisiana
Present day, three months before the fire

Landry Drake didn't invite anyone to his swearing-in ceremony. If he'd been joining the police force in a city like Baton Rouge or Shreveport, there might have been other graduates, a speech by the police chief, and a recitation of solemn promises with one hand on the Bible. But it wasn't that way today.

He became an Iberia Parish deputy sheriff in his boss's office. Instead of hearing his name called and walking across a stage to receive his credentials, the sheriff handed him a badge and a belt that contained everything an officer should need — pepper spray, a taser, handcuffs, service revolver, baton, two-way radio and a punch for breaking car windows.

Congratulations, he said to himself, because no one else did. He hadn't given law enforcement any thought, but after graduating from a small college with a degree in journalism, he came home to Jeanerette, moved in with his folks, and began looking for work. The first in his family to attend college, he received little encouragement from two parents who worked long shifts for low wages. He soon found that jobs were scarce and his degree was useless. The only thing people did with a print journalism degree was to work for a newspaper for low pay in a dying industry. The paper in New Iberia had no openings anyway, so he took a job in a bar while he waited for something else.

Landry had worked long shifts at the Cajun Corner for over a year. Then he saw a job posting — the sheriff's office was hiring. As a deputy, he'd make twenty dollars an hour and have good benefits, including paid time off. For a twenty-five-year-old, it was perfect. He got the job and went to a CLEET facility for several months of training, followed by more months of OJT. Today, one year later, he got his badge.

Iberia Parish covered almost six hundred square miles, and there were only two deputies on duty at night. Landry had to drive the rural roads for six hours, and he struggled to stay awake during each mind-numbing shift. The cruiser didn't have an AM/FM radio, and he wasn't allowed to listen to music on his phone. He had to stay alert for transmissions from the deputy on duty back at headquarters, but nothing exciting ever happened. Every hour, the patrol deputies had to check in by radio. After that came fifty-nine and a half minutes of dead time.

For the first few weeks he hoped for something to break the monotony, but he gave up. Nights in a rural parish were quiet, and as a deputy, that was what he should want. But it was boring as hell. Between interminable stretches of doing nothing, he investigated noises around people's houses, jump-started dead batteries, and kept an eye on farm buildings when owners were out of town. Now and then there was a "crime," almost always involving a tipsy driver. At first he hauled offenders to town, booked them, and put them in the drunk tank, but the paperwork took longer than the time the guys stayed in jail. Plus, Landry had to appear in court and sometimes sit for hours, all on his own time. Why arrest someone who just needed to go home to bed?

He still hauled in the belligerent, knee-walking drunks. He let the rest go with a stern warning and often followed them until they were safely home. Now and then, he even drove them himself. Having grown up in this parish, he knew some of these people, and he sympathized with their plight. Hell, he'd been there himself back in high school. He'd have spent the night in the drunk tank — and gotten a beating from his dad — if some cop hadn't given him a break.

Out on the back roads of the parish one night, he did his hourly check-in with another deputy back at the office, and on a whim, he drove to Victory. He could explain away his presence there if he had to. It was in the parish and within his jurisdiction, even if nobody lived there. He hadn't been to the Asylum in twelve years, and he wondered if the old building was still there. Avoiding potholes and crumbling asphalt, he drove down Main Street and turned left onto Iberia Avenue, named for the once-famous hotel at its end. The ShopRite convenience store on the right had been closed for years; he remembered his brother having bought a Coke there when he was at the Asylum as a kid. A mile down the road, he came to the brick wall that encircled the prison grounds.

He saw the concrete sign. There was spray paint on it, but the words were clear.

Victory Institution for the Criminally Insane.

It was as easy to pass through the entry gate tonight as the time before. He drove past the partly collapsed gatehouse where a hundred years ago, armed guards would have been on duty around the clock. Sentries weren't needed anymore. The place was dark, foreboding and empty.

Hopefully.

Landry stopped his patrol car in front of the four-story structure. He shivered, recalling the terror he'd felt when he'd last gone inside twelve years ago. He might not be a kid anymore, but that afternoon of horror would forever be etched into his memory. He'd been an impressionable teenager who fainted when something touched him.

Shrugging off the shivers, he lightly rested his hand on his pistol as he walked up the stairs and across the broad porch.

He didn't believe the stories, but the place was spooky as hell. He still felt goosebumps and a sense of uneasiness as he entered the main room. There was more graffiti now, and the stench of urine and feces was everywhere.

On the way here, he'd set a goal to walk down that hallway and find his name on the wall. Now that he was inside, listening to the same groans and whistling noises as the wind rustled through broken windowpanes, he wasn't sure he could do it.

Come on, Landry. You're a cop now, for God's sake.

He took out his pistol and flashlight and stepped into the long hallway. There was a lot of trash — people were squatting in here, and he wondered why the owner allowed it. Who was he, and why had he let the place go to ruin?

He found his name on the wall. He looked at it as memories from that rainy afternoon flooded his mind. Something had brushed against him, and the memory gave him chills.

A voice came from somewhere behind him. He recoiled and raised his pistol.

"Who is it?" It was a girl's voice. Tentative, soft and quiet, nestled among the whispers of the wind. "Is someone there?"

He shined his light into the cells across the hall. The sense of foreboding swept over him just as it had twelve years ago on this very spot. He felt woozy.

That was a real voice you heard. Concentrate, Landry.

"Police!" he shouted. "Is someone there?"

"Don't shoot!" A dirty, emaciated teenager emerged from a cell with her hands in the air. She wore a flimsy T-shirt and shorts, and as he put the light on her, he could see track marks on her arms.

"What are you doing here?"

"We were just looking for someplace to sleep, my boyfriend and me. We didn't mean no harm, officer."

"Where's your boyfriend?"

She pointed to the cell behind her. "He's in there. He passed out a while ago."

"How long have you all been here?" Landry was unsure what to do, and he asked more questions as he tried to come up with something.

"Just since yesterday, sir. We didn't mean no harm."

He felt sorry for the girl. She couldn't have been more than eighteen, and she looked pathetic and desperate.

"Where did you get your drugs?"

"I dunno. Some guy. We hitchhiked here from New Mexico and scored some shit in some little town. The guy said people crashed at this place sometimes, so we came here."

There was no point in arresting the pair. He'd have to call for backup and deal with the comatose boyfriend, and he'd have to explain why he'd come all the way out here on nightly rounds. It wasn't like she was causing any trouble.

"When's the last time you ate?"

"I dunno. Maybe yesterday or the day before. Like I said, Bobby and me spent our money scoring some shit, and when I'm high, I don't get hungry."

Landry reached in his pocket, pulled out a twenty, and said, "Promise me you'll use this for food."

"So you're gonna let me go?"

"Yes," he said, "but I want you all to clear out of here in the morning. You're trespassing, and this place is dangerous."

"We're not the only ones in here. There are others. Not people. Scary things."

His skin prickled. "What do you mean by that?"

"Up there." She pointed toward the ceiling fifteen feet above, where peeling paint hung in strips. "See them?"

Wispy, filmy things hovered high above like gossamer webs. Almost invisible, they shifted and floated as though wafting in a breeze, although the air was quiet and still. They were moving on their own. He remembered them well.

"They say things. I heard their voices. The building has lots of sounds, but they say words. I don't know where they are or who they are, and I don't want to know. We're just minding our own business, know what I mean? I don't want to mess with those things."

"What do the voices say?"

"Mostly they're asking for help. They're real sad voices, you know? I know me and Bobby are strung out, but I swear I heard them. Listen! There's one now!"

Help me! Help me!

The same words he had heard twelve years ago. The same lost, hopeless words.

"I've got to make rounds," he mumbled, embarrassed at his nervousness. "You'll leave tomorrow — promise?"

"Yes, sir. We'll be gone, I promise. Thanks for giving us a break. And, officer, I need to know something. You did hear the words, right? You heard someone asking for help?"

He walked away without answering. As he turned onto the main road, he tried to convince himself that he had done the right thing. He didn't know that girl. He didn't owe her an answer. And he hoped she'd be all right.

He wasn't sure what he'd heard that day anyway. It didn't matter; for now, like before, he just wanted to be as far from this place as possible. Like the last time, he had a frightening realization that there were strange forces at work inside the abandoned prison. Things — unearthly things —

inhabited the Asylum. Not vagrants or squatters. Not trespassers. Something different.

He had an idea — a crazy thought — about what those strands of nothingness were. Although he wasn't religious, he thought they were the souls of inmates, the victims of unspeakable horrors. Once they had been men — violent criminals imprisoned there over a hundred years ago — and even in death they couldn't escape from what had happened to them in that hellish madhouse.

The Asylum was dark and forbidding. The place frightened him, but Landry wanted to know more. Something that common sense and rationality couldn't explain was going on inside those walls. He had to find out what.

CHAPTER FIVE

Every so often, Landry got a break from driving the rural roads for endless hours. Instead, he took a shift in the office, manning the phone and radio and keeping an eye on occupants of the jail. He looked forward to the change because at last he had something to do — he could surf the web. He began by researching cold cases in Iberia Parish. He thought he might find something interesting to pass the time, and not long afterwards, he did.

In 2012, fraternity brothers at a nearby college gave three pledges a task as part of Hell Week and initiation. They were taken to the Asylum at midnight and ordered to stay inside the building until dawn. The brothers said they would be nearby to make sure the pledges didn't leave, but in reality they went home to sleep.

The next morning, two members of Alpha Gamma fraternity drove through the front gates of the institution and saw its gothic turrets dark against the early morning sky. As they walked across the decaying porch, they heard a horrifying scream from somewhere inside. Thinking it was a prank, they laughed and jeered.

As they approached the dark space where the front door had once hung, a pledge staggered out, holding his hands to his chest. His shirt was soaked in blood, and he stared blankly at what looked like stab wounds in his chest.

"Jason," one of the brothers shouted mockingly, "you're not scaring anyone. Good try and great bloodstains, but it's time to go home."

The pledge didn't respond. He swayed, fell forward and hit the floor. Alarmed, the brothers ran to him and turned him over.

"He's ... he's dead!"

"He can't be dead! They're playing some kind of trick!"

"There's no pulse. No breathing. He's dead! God, what are we going to do?"

"Oh shit!" one said, pointing toward the open door that the mortally wounded pledge had walked through. A ray of sunlight pierced the windows, bringing light into a large room.

"What do you see?" the other asked, peering into the gloom. He pointed upwards. "What's that?"

An enormous old brass chandelier hung from the fourteen-foot ceiling. The lifeless body of pledge number two swayed back and forth from one of its arms.

"It's Darrell. God, it's Darrell. He's hanged himself!"

One ran inside, leaving his friend throwing up on the porch. Dangling from a noose, his feet swaying four feet above the floor, was one of their pledges.

"Call 911! Call the cops!"

Another hideous, awful scream came from somewhere, and then they heard the voice of the last pledge.

"Help me! Don't! Please don't! Oh, God! He's coming! He's —"

Then there was nothing. Nothing but terror everywhere.

"Run! Get out of here!" the one who'd gone inside screamed as he joined his friend on the porch.

Two hours later, the Asylum was swarming with investigators. The coroner sat in his van in the old prison parking lot, waiting for crime scene investigators to finish up. He'd called for a second van because his wasn't large enough to transport three bodies.

A detective interrogated the two fraternity brothers, took their statements, and sent them away. They were guilty of trespassing, but he was certain they had nothing to do with the murders. Once he checked out their backgrounds, he'd find they were all from good families, made good grades, and had never been in trouble. These college students didn't commit these atrocious crimes. Their only mistake had been to send kids into a building where a frenzied killer waited.

One boy had died from asphyxiation due to hanging. Someone hauled him up there while he was alive, investigators noted, because he couldn't have gotten up that high by himself. The other two pledges were fatally stabbed. The third boy — the one the fraternity men heard shouting — had died last. They had arrived just as the killer was doing his work somewhere in the back of the building.

The police thought the perp was a man — maybe two. The dying pledge's last word had been *he*, and it took strength to hoist what had to have been a struggling, husky youth up to the crossbar of the chandelier and hang him.

Landry continued his search and was surprised to learn that several trespassers had been murdered there over the years.

Everybody said the Asylum was haunted, and the more his list of victims grew, the more Landry believed it. As a kid, he had heard more scary tales about this place than anywhere else around, and that was saying a lot, since there were plenty of ghost stories in Cajun country.

Landry had a hard time manipulating the data. All he wanted to see were crimes at the old prison. He could sort data using several criteria, but not by location. It took time to do it manually, but time was something he had. He scrolled backwards through the years and wrote down each crime. Every one was an unsolved murder.

The online database went back to 1980. Landry learned that between that year and 1988 there were no criminal incidents at the Asylum. But between 1989 and today — not counting the fraternity pledges five years ago — nine men and one woman had died either in the massive old building or on the grounds. Including the boys, there had been thirteen. Astonished, he wondered if anyone else had ever connected the dots. There was no way that thirteen unexplained deaths in one place could be a coincidence.

When his shift was over the next morning, Landry waited for Sheriff Barbour to arrive. He revealed what he had found, and his boss was not happy. He said if Landry didn't have enough to do on the night shift, he had plenty of chores to keep him occupied.

The sheriff explained, "I know there are unsolved crimes, but other than those fraternity boys, the victims were druggies, every one of 'em. It's always drug related, and they're always murdered by their own kind. They squat in the building, claim their space and get into fights if someone tries to take over their territory. They get high, they get stabbed, they die, and sometimes nobody even claims the bodies. Yes, the cases are still open, but I guarantee they're sure as hell not unsolved mysteries. Let it go, Landry. This isn't what I hired you to do."

Landry tried to explain. The curious thing, he said, was that nine of the thirteen weren't necessarily murdered at all. The medical examiner said the cause of death was unknown.

"How does that work, Sheriff? How can a coroner have nine bodies from the same location but he can't conclusively say how any of them died? It doesn't make sense."

"Hell if I know, son, but I know one thing. When there's investigating to be done, the state police handle it. I'm not running a detective agency, and you're not Sherlock Holmes. I'm ordering you to let it go."

Landry persisted. "Even two or three deaths would be a pattern, and over twenty-eight years there have been thirteen. The fraternity deaths happened five years ago. Have the state police come down here one time since then to work on that case? I'll bet money they haven't."

The sheriff's face turned red. "Landry, listen to me. You're way out of line here. I'm only going to tell you this one more time. It's not my job to second-guess the state investigators, and I'd just as soon they stay up in Baton Rouge than mess around in my parish. I don't care if the causes of death are unknown. None of the dead people except the college boys had families. Nobody gives a damn about the cases anymore. Let it go. Go home and get some sleep."

Landry went home, but sleep didn't come. *He* gave a damn about the cases. Something was wrong out in that old building, and he was determined to learn what it was.

CHAPTER SIX

What I do on my own time is my business, Landry rationalized as he paid two dollars to the Iberia Parish county clerk to copy a deed. Now he knew that the former prison's owner was Madison John Adams of Galveston, who had bought it in 2012. He googled the name and learned that Adams was a psychiatrist and somewhat of a celebrity among his peers. He spoke at national conferences in his field and had written dozens of articles in medical journals.

Why does a doctor in Galveston own an old prison complex in Iberia Parish?

He found the phone number for Adams's clinic. Before he could talk himself out of it, he dialed.

"Adams Psychiatry Group. This is Cate. How may I help you?"

Why the hell didn't I think what I was going to say before I called?

"Uh, this is Landry Drake. I'm ... uh, I'm with the sheriff's department in Iberia Parish, Louisiana."

She interrupted. "The sheriff's department? Is something wrong?"

"No, nothing like that. I'm looking into a crime that happened at the former prison in Victory a few years ago. I learned that Dr. Adams owns the building. Is this his office?"

"Hold on." She was gone for a few seconds and then returned to the line. This time her words were curt and sharp. "I can talk more freely now. This is Cate Adams. I'm Dr. Adams's daughter. What's the reason for your call, Sheriff Drake?"

Uh-oh. Better be careful. You don't want her calling the sheriff.

"Yes, ma'am. Uh, no, ma'am, like I said, there's no problem at all. Yes, I'm Landry Drake. I'm not the sheriff — I'm a deputy. I was just checking on something —"

She cut him off. "Is this about the fraternity murders? That happened five years ago. My father gave a statement to the police. Is there a new development?"

Anything he said could drive him deeper into a situation that could cost him his job, but he wanted to learn more about what he'd found online.

"Please don't be alarmed, Miss Adams. It's not the fraternity murders. There were several other unsolved crimes long before your father owned the property. This has nothing to do with him. I'm just checking to see if there's any connection."

"This doesn't make sense. I don't believe you. You're after something from my father. This isn't about his property at all. If I call the sheriff's office in New Iberia, will they have even heard of you, Landry Drake?"

He couldn't blame her. These days, people had to be careful. He drew in a deep breath of air and replied, "Miss Adams, I really am a deputy sheriff, and you're free to call the office and confirm that. If you want to tell them about this call, you're free to do that too, but please listen to me for a moment. I've researched crimes at the Asylum over the past thirty years, and I came across several unsolved murders. Thirteen, Miss Adams. Twelve men and a woman died at the prison since 1988. Don't you think that sounds like a lot?"

"So you're reopening these cases?"

"No," he admitted. "In fact, my boss told me to leave all this alone. Stop worrying about a bunch of vagrants killed by other vagrants is what he told me. But I can't stop thinking about it. Thirteen people have died there over thirty years. That's unusual, and I think they deserve to have someone find out why. You were right earlier; I am working on my own, but I want to know more."

Her voice softened. "If that's what you're really about, then I'd have to agree with you. I don't know you or if you're telling the truth. If your story checks out, I'll be back in touch." She hung up.

He fretted for the two hours it took her to call.

"When can you meet me?" she asked.

"I work nights. I'm off days and also Thursday and Friday nights. Do you want me to come to Galveston?"

"Pick me up at the Lafayette airport at 10:45 Friday morning."

"You don't have to come here —"

"If you want any information from our family, I do. I'm not telling you anything until I meet you and see for myself what this is about. If I trust you, we'll go to the Asylum, and I'll fly back later that afternoon."

"Great! I'll pick you up."

On Friday, she exited the security area, looked for a purple and gold LSU ball cap, and saw a nice-looking guy in his mid-twenties, only a year or so older than she was. He hadn't known what to expect, but as she walked toward him he saw a beautiful girl with raven-black hair pulled back into a ponytail, wearing a white long-sleeved shirt, jeans and tall boots. She carried a long cardboard tube, which she explained held copies of the Asylum's original floor plan.

"I'm in short-term parking. Let's go through here," he pointed, but she shook her head.

"Not quite yet. I want to see your driver's license and your badge."

That's a smart move, he thought as he handed both over to her. She gave them a quick glance and handed them back. "Okay, I'm ready to go. I wasn't getting in the car with someone who claimed to be Landry Drake but ended up being Jack the Ripper."

He smiled and said he completely understood.

They chatted on the forty-five-minute drive to Victory. She told him she'd called the sheriff's office and confirmed he worked there. "And don't worry. Your secret's safe. That's all I asked. They don't even know who I was."

"Thanks. My boss might have gotten upset if you'd said why you were coming over here."

She wanted to know everything. He said he had gone to the courthouse to examine the records before 1980, the year the online database began. Several hundred people had died on the property between 1875 and 1907, when it was a prison. The vast majority of deaths were between inmates. It must have been a horrible place, he said, and he wondered how many of the deceased were actually murdered by guards.

Between 1907 and 1980, only a few people had died on the property. All of those cases were still open and unsolved, but no one had looked into them in years, according to the information Landry found.

It surprised her that there had been deaths after the place closed. "How did those people die?" she asked.

"As I recall, there were a couple of brutal stabbings and a hanging, but the others were listed as unknown. I thought one was interesting. They found a body back in the 1930s and the coroner wrote 'Probably died of fright.'"

"Fright? How can a coroner put that as the official reason someone died? He can't get into a person's mind."

"I asked the same question. He had to conclude something to wrap things up, and he took the easy way out. People around here invented lots of tall tales about Victory and the old prison. Your father owns what people say is the most haunted building in the state."

"I know all about the ghosts." She laughed. "I'll tell you about my dad and the spooky stories later. But tell me more about what you found out."

"Okay. Where did I leave off? So a few people died before 1980. From then until 1988, nothing happened, but then the mysterious deaths started again. Ten more happened between 1989 and 2011. Your dad bought the building in 2012, and there was that awful case of the three fraternity pledges later that year."

"You've put a lot of work into this. I'm impressed."

"Once I got started, it was hard to stop. I grew up in Jeanerette, just five miles from Victory. Like everyone else, I heard ghost stories all my life about the place and the mysterious happenings out at the old insane asylum-slash-prison. Have you been there since your father bought it? And speaking of that, can you tell me why in the world a doctor in Texas wanted an abandoned prison in a ghost town?"

"I don't blame you for wondering. To answer your first question, I have been to the Asylum before, but it was a long time ago — way before Dad bought it. He brought us to southern Louisiana a lot when I was a kid. My parents loved the charm of this area and the history of the Acadians. If somebody said a plantation was haunted, that was even better. He loves ghost stories, unexplained mysteries and tales of Civil War battles. I loved his enthusiasm, and Mom did too, even though she pretended to be upset when he hauled us through antebellum mansions looking for ghosts.

"I've had the bejeezus scared out of me a dozen times while walking through empty houses, hearing strange noises, imagining what was making those sounds, and listening to my dad's stories. He painted mental pictures of gracious Southern ladies shooting Union soldiers dead on grand staircases and servants defending the house as the damned Yankees set fire to it.

"Dad loves what-ifs. He loves to imagine what might have happened in a certain place, but to a little girl, some of the things he told me — and the spooky places where I was standing when he dreamed up those stories — scared the hell out of me, to be honest."

Landry laughed; he was already enjoying his time with this vivacious, attractive girl very much. He checked her left hand — no ring, but that didn't mean no attachments. It was far too early to be thinking those thoughts, he reminded himself. He knew nothing about her.

"So your dad bought the Asylum because it was haunted?"

Cate burst out laughing. "I guess that's the logical conclusion after what I told you. And that could have been his ulterior motive. Dad's been buying tax liens, surplus government property and foreclosures for years. He owns hundreds of properties, and he's made a lot of money at it. He attended an auction in Baton Rouge one Saturday to look for bargains, and he picked up a few repos. There was a sale of surplus property owned by the state that afternoon, and he found out the thirty acres on the bayou — the old prison — was on the list.

"We'd been there, like I said, but it was a long time ago. He wasn't sure about bidding on this property. He didn't mind paying low prices for old houses or vacant property, but this was a different story. The annual taxes alone on the Asylum were more than he'd paid for all the properties he'd bought that morning. He decided to watch the auction and see how things went."

Landry nodded. "From what little you've said, I'll bet he was interested in the Asylum's history and its ghosts."

"Way more than making money flipping the old building. He's a sucker for ghost stories, that's for sure. Anyway, the auctioneer opened the bidding at four hundred thousand and got no bidders. Dad said the man worked the crowd hard, but nobody seemed interested, so he raised his paddle and offered two thousand dollars."

"Wow! That's a far cry from four hundred thousand!"

"It was an absolute auction. There was no minimum bid and no reserve, and no one else wanted it. My father got the property for two grand."

"That's amazing!"

"Not if you think about it. Why were there no other bidders? Because it's worthless. It's an old prison in a ghost town. If Victory still had a city council, they would have condemned it a long time ago. It's a safety hazard and an eyesore, but nobody lives in Victory, so nobody cares. And who wants to buy something that you have to spend a fortune on? Say Dad spent twenty thousand tearing down the building. What would he have then? Thirty acres on the bayou that aren't worth what he spent. See what I mean? It's not worth anything. The state should have torn it down and sold the land for whatever they could gct. But they didn't, and my dad ended up with a building full of ghosts. Too bad Hitchcock's not alive. He'd have loved the story!"

"Speaking of which, here's our turnoff," he said, taking an exit off Highway 90. Moments later they drove along Main Street through what was left of downtown Victory. On the other side of town, he came to an old highway sign that read "Prison, One Mile" with an arrow pointing to the left. He turned onto Iberia Avenue, drove a mile, and went through the archway past the guardhouse. Cate gasped at the dark, sinister building, its empty windows gaping like blank eyes and yawning mouths.

"I'd forgotten how this place scared me. Some of my dad's vacation spots were nice, but more were like this. We went lots of places, but nothing ever scared me as much as that building in front of us. I first saw it when I was maybe seven or eight. The place looked just like it does now, but it was way more frightening, because I was a kid and Dad told me about the ghosts that roamed the halls at night. I'm twenty-three years old, and I'm as nervous right now as when I first came here. How crazy is that?"

"It's not crazy at all. I'm uneasy too. This could be part of a horror movie set. But if it scares you, why did you agree to come? We didn't have to do this."

"I'm a grown woman. I'm too old to be afraid of ghosts. You're a deputy sheriff who's investigating the place. My family owns it. Why shouldn't I be able to walk through it with you?"

As he parked, he said, "I have a confession. This is my third visit."

"Really? When were you here?"

"The first time was when I was thirteen. When you said a minute ago how scared you were at seven or eight, it brought back a lot of memories. My brother dared me to spend an hour here, and I have to admit it was the most terrifying thing I have ever been through."

She laughed. "Yeah, kids can be impressionable, especially in a creepy old place like this. When was the second time?"

"Two or three weeks ago. I was trespassing, and I'm sorry. When I was doing nightly rounds in the parish, I decided to see how much the place had changed."

"You weren't trespassing. You're a cop with every right to check out abandoned properties. Did you go inside?"

"Yeah. I scared the hell out of myself and some strung-out teenaged girl. I felt sorry for her. She and her boyfriend were sleeping in there because they'd spent whatever money they had on drugs. I gave her a little cash and told them to clear out the next morning."

"You didn't arrest them?"

"No. I decided it wouldn't have done anyone any good. They meant no harm, and like I said, I felt sorry for the girl. She needed way more help than I could provide, and spending the night in a cell wasn't the answer either."

"Did you notice anything strange that night — other than the people, I mean?"

He chose his words carefully. "There were sounds. The girl said they heard voices, but I wasn't sure."

"Did you hear something?"

"I heard something, but the building makes all kinds of noises, and the wind whistles through the broken windows upstairs. She said someone was calling for help, but I'm not sure."

He had told her a lie. He was sure. He was certain he'd heard the same words the girl had.

Cate smiled, glad that she was here with Landry. She had liked him when they met, and now she liked him even more. There was something genuine about him — he seemed to care about other people. That was a rare trait, at least in the guys she'd dated.

Landry opened the car door and stepped out. "Okay, Miss Adams! Are you ready?"

"My name's Catherine, but call me Cate. Yes, I guess I'm ready." She shook off another shudder. "This place still gives me the creeps!"

Me too.

She suggested they look at the floor plans before going in. She took several large sheets from the cardboard tube and spread them on the hood of his SUV.

"Where on earth did you get these?"

"Dad found them in the historical museum in New Orleans. He had them copied, and when I told him I was coming here, he said they might come in handy. These are the plans Frank Connolly had drawn up before he built the hotel in 1820."

Landry looked at the first page. Ornate scrollwork in one corner surrounded a legend identifying this drawing as "Hotel Iberia, Victory, Louisiana. Plate I: Grand Salon and First Floor. Labat and Sons, Architects, New Orleans. 1819." The fascinating drawings were a slice of Louisiana history.

"I'll bet it thrilled your dad to find these! They're like stepping back two hundred years. Was there anything in here that surprised him?"

"After he got the plans, he walked the building with them in his hands. He said there were a lot of peculiarities. There were rooms and basements on the plan that he couldn't find.

Dad said before the time of modern conveniences like electricity and hot running water, hotels would have had underground rooms to store perishables.

"The kitchen is a separate building behind the main structure, and it's still there today. There once was an underground passage running two hundred feet from the kitchen to a room below the hotel. Dad looked, but he couldn't find any of that. He figured the authorities destroyed them when the place became a prison, so it couldn't be used as an escape route. Let me show you."

She flipped back through the large sheets and found a map of the grounds that indicated something — perhaps a tunnel — running across the yard between the two buildings. There was no description of it, and Landry thought maybe it hadn't been underground at all. It might have been a walkway, an aboveground covered path that the servants used to take food back and forth. There might not have been basements in either building.

She laughed and said she'd keep his theories to herself. She had no intention of challenging her dad's ideas about ghostly passageways somewhere beneath his ancient insane asylum. "He loves thinking about what might have been, and at the least he makes his theories exciting!"

She pointed out other buildings that no longer stood. A cellblock had once stood behind the main building, but today only the foundation remained. Likewise, thirteen small structures near the back of the property had housed the hotel's servants. Those little houses were gone too.

They walked onto the broad porch, pausing in front of the gaping entrance and peering into the darkness.

"When the hotel opened, it must have been quite a place," he said. Even in disrepair, with doors and windows long gone, one could imagine its former grandeur.

She continued talking, apparently in no hurry to go inside. "Every time my dad planned a trip to one of his crazy places, he would do a lot of research so he could give my mother and me a history lesson. This place was something special. He really outdid himself when he brought Mom and me here. The stories about this place really caught his attention.

"From what he told us, I agree with you that it must have been an amazing place in the 1820s. The Hotel Iberia was where rich people from all around gathered for lunch and socializing. There were deaths way back then too. One story that sticks in my mind involves Frank Connolly, the rich guy who built the hotel. He was in his sixties when it opened, and according to legend, one of the chambermaids became pregnant by him in 1824. She was eighteen and African-American, and she thought he loved her. When she learned the sad truth, she climbed to the turret — that one, right up there — and jumped to her death. I can't imagine the shock when she hit the ground right in front of the guests who were enjoying drinks on the veranda." She pointed to a spot in the front yard and added, "Her body would have landed right about there."

"What a story! Is it true?"

"Dad spun a lot of stories, but that one happened. It was the first unexplained death, although the authorities wrapped it up quickly. A servant who took her own life apparently wasn't worthy of much attention back then. Dad wasn't surprised when he considered that Mr. Connolly was a prosperous man, mayor of the town, and the owner of the finest establishment for miles around. Connolly's affluent guests spent money in Victory too. Because of him everyone benefitted, and the townspeople revered him. There was no reason to irritate the wealthiest man in the parish by looking into a death that nobody cared about anyway. It's unfortunate, but that's how things were two hundred years ago."

At last she walked inside, and Landry followed. "This was the lobby," she said, waving her arm around the vast, high-ceilinged gloomy room. "It would have been beautiful, although that's hard to imagine now."

When Frank Connolly's hotel had become a prison, everything ornate and fancy had been stripped out. This once-elegant lobby had become the prison's reception area, the only place visitors were allowed. Cate explained that this room would have had a waiting area and lots of desks for clerks and administrative personnel.

At the far end there were cubicles with walls about six feet high. They looked out of place in an enormous room with twenty-foot ceilings. "Those were offices for the warden, his deputies and the others who ran this place."

"When families came to visit prisoners, where did that happen?"

She shook her head with a rueful smile. "There was no need for a visiting room here. No one ever came to see these men, because visiting wasn't allowed. Most prisoners never had a moment of social interaction unless you counted the guy who pushed the food through a slot in their cell doors twice a day. A few inmates — the ones who behaved and didn't act like the psychotic sociopaths they were — spent an hour a week outdoors in a ten-foot-square cage. They were the lucky ones. There was a hose out there they used for a shower. The others almost never got out of their cells."

Landry was amazed at the barbarity. "How did those guys bathe?"

"They didn't. You can't imagine how this place must have smelled. They used the bathroom in their cells in chamber pots that got emptied once a day … if they behaved. The ones who didn't — the belligerent ones or screamers or men who went into fits of rage — those prisoners lived in their own filth for days at a time. For normal people, it's impossible to comprehend what went on inside these walls."

"There are metal toilets in some of the cells. I saw them when I was here before."

"Those were added later, and only a few cells had them. I have no idea which category of inmate got the special privilege of having a commode to sit on."

She paused, listening.

There was a sound from somewhere in the bowels of the building.

"What was that?"

"I don't know. Listen! There it is again!"

There was a muffled scraping noise followed by a distinct *thump*.

Cate grabbed his arm tightly and moved closer. "What is it?" she whispered. "Is someone else in here?"

"Let's find out." He shouted, "Deputy sheriff! Who's there?"

They heard creaks and cracks, the sounds an old building makes. But that was all. No scrapes, no thumps.

"I'll check it out," he said, wanting to appear brave. The noises made him nervous, and since his arm was in the viselike grip of Cate's hand, he knew she was scared too. "Wait here for me." He drew his service revolver.

"No way! I'm not staying here by myself."

He took a flashlight from his belt and they walked across the room, pausing at the doorway that led back into the darkness. Above the door, the "No Visitors" sign Landry had first seen as a kid still hung askew. He gently removed her hand from his arm and took it in his and switched on his light. They went into the corridor.

He helped her maneuver around piles of debris as they passed the doors on both sides of the wide corridor. These once were lavishly appointed hotel suites, she commented, adding that when the rooms were divided into cells, the doors became gateways to hellish cubicles where inmates were confined for months or years. Landry thought of the difference between the good years, when occupants of these rooms were treated like royalty, and the later years, when they were treated worse than dogs.

He kept those thoughts to himself as he pointed out places along the floor where boards were missing, so she wouldn't trip. Halfway down the hall, he showed her his scrawled name and the date from twelve years ago. They walked to the back and came to another wall of bars in the back. This time they couldn't go on because the old gate was still in place, its hinges rusted shut.

He'd never been this far into the old building, and he asked if there was another way to get upstairs. She nodded and led him back into the front room, thankful for the light streaming through the huge front windows.

She pointed to a far corner of the room. "There's a stairway behind that door."

Landry opened the door. There was a moldy odor, and he created a cloud of dust that startled them. The room was the size of a coat closet and contained a metal stairway that wound upward around a center pole. The tight stairs filled the tiny room completely.

"This couldn't have been the hotel's original staircase. I expected something ornate and showy."

Cate explained that there had been a thirty-foot-wide marble stairway that swept up from the main room — the lobby back then — to salons on the second floor. Contractors tore it down when they converted the building to a prison.

"When this was a hotel," she added, "ladies in fancy ball gowns would have descended the marble staircase like the queen greeting her subjects. Dad showed me pictures of what it looked like back then. When he found the original floor plans, he also found records from when they converted the building, and that's how he knew what happened to the original stairway.

"The prison officials chose functionality over grandeur. The tiny circular stairway was behind a locked door, and it was for the guards only. There was another stairway in the back of the building for maintenance people and the like. The prisoners used that one too, at least the ones allowed out in the pen behind the building for an hour a week."

He played the flashlight all around, up and down. Then he knelt and directed the beam along the risers.

Standing behind him in the cramped stairwell, Cate couldn't see what he was doing. "Have you found something?"

He stepped to one side and handed her the flashlight. "Look at that."

"They're footprints."

They were a man's boot prints. Someone had recently walked up these stairs.

"Is someone up there?" she asked him. No one had the right to be here except them, but if someone surprised them upstairs, rights wouldn't matter.

"I don't hear anything, but I'll do whatever you say. Want to go up?"

"Do you?"

He nodded and patted his pistol. In a more confident tone than he felt inside, he said, "We came here to see the building. If you're game, so am I."

"Aren't you just a little nervous?"

He smiled at her candor. He liked this girl already.

"Nervous isn't the word for it. This place gives me the creeps."

CHAPTER SEVEN

Guards once would have unlocked a steel door to get from the staircase to each floor, but the doors and their frames were gone now. Landry and Cate went to the fourth floor and walked into a wide hallway that ran the length of the building. She pointed to a doorway at the far end that led to a covered porch. When this was a hotel, couples would have enjoyed their afternoon tea or evening cocktails al fresco. Now, both that doorway and all the windows still had bars that must have been too secure for vandals to destroy.

What had once been hotel rooms along the corridor had been split into tiny cells. There was detritus everywhere, evidence that people had squatted in the massive old structure, but it appeared they were the only ones in the building now.

Although the day was bright and sunny, it was as though any warmth was blocked by the gothic turrets on each corner of the Asylum. Even on the top floor, the steel bars over each window seemed to act as barriers, keeping beauty, breezes and sunlight outdoors where they belonged. Landry mentioned how unfriendly — maybe even hostile — the old prison felt, as though it had a malevolent personality of its own.

She agreed. "I've always felt uneasy about this place. But a building can't be evil. That's not possible. I think what happened here is a buildup of negative energy. Do you know what I'm saying?"

"I'm not sure."

Her father had spent a lot of time researching this old building's past. The prison opened in 1875, and from the very beginning it was a place to sweep problems under the rug. They dumped hundreds of inmates here because they were too hard to handle. If you were psychotic, full of rage, a danger to guards or other inmates, or if you pissed off the wrong corrections officer, you took a one-way ride to Victory.

This prison was different. Rehabilitation programs, psychiatric and medical care, training on how to return to society — none of those things was offered at the Asylum. State officials kept quiet about it, but the truth was that the owners were paid to make the state's problems go away. These inmates were never going back into society. They were written off, and the guards here were allowed to do anything they wanted to them.

"The things Dad learned were more horrifying than any ghost story. Over eight hundred inmates were incarcerated from 1875 until 1907. Guess how many of them died here."

Landry guessed maybe half.

"All but twelve. In thirty-two years, just twelve men were released. Each one of them had an 'accident.' They fell down the stairs, broke their necks, suffered concussions — stuff like that. They were seriously injured. It was expensive to care for them, so they were released and became someone else's problem.

"Dad learned a lot. He doesn't think people 'fell down the stairs.' He thinks the guards beat the hell out of them. Those twelve guys that were released just happened to survive. Almost all the rest were murdered by men who worked here. The guards were as bad as the inmates, maybe worse. According to my father, over three hundred bodies are buried in the prison cemetery. Where the rest went, nobody knows. I guess their families claimed them."

"My God, what a horrible place! I had no idea all that happened here."

"It was a well-kept secret. Dad said he had a heck of a time finding information, and a lot of what he thinks happened, he put together from bits and pieces in old letters and the stuff he found in New Orleans. When this place closed in 1907, most of the records were conveniently destroyed in a fire. Dad went up to Baton Rouge a few months ago and met with the corrections director. He offered his theories, and the man agreed he might be right. You can't prove anything because what happened here was covered up."

Amazed they could have gotten away with it, Landry stood in the hallway and had a powerful feeling that there was unfinished business in this place. It was no surprise that malevolence was in the air. The very building they were in was evil. Bad things had happened within these walls. Men caged like animals had experienced unimaginable horrors. Hundreds of forgotten men had died here.

For nearly one hundred years, this awful place had been abandoned.

Abandoned, but only by the living. The living were gone, but the dead remained. He could feel their presence, just like the other times he was here.

Landry was right. There was unfinished business in this awful place.

CHAPTER EIGHT

Mackey Thorn had lived around this part of southern Louisiana for all of his sixty-three years except for a couple of stints behind bars. His elderly grandparents had ended up raising a kid they'd never liked, and they resented having to take care of Mack instead of growing old by themselves. Predictably, he didn't do well in school. Intelligence wasn't the issue; he simply didn't care. School administrators couldn't get through to him, and his grandparents were too old and too unconcerned to do anything. The teachers at his school kept an eye on Mack because they thought he would explode someday.

From first grade he'd been a bully, but as he grew in age, stature and reputation, he became a sadistic thug. Thanks to flunking two grades in elementary school, he was a big, strong thirteen-year-old in the fifth grade — a testosterone-ravaged six-footer who terrorized and oppressed students and teachers alike. Discussing the incorrigible child in the teacher's lounge, his instructors gave him a nickname that stuck for a lifetime. Mad Mack, they called him behind his back. Mad as in crazy, or mad as in furious. Take your pick, they laughed uneasily. Either one described the boy perfectly.

He spent most of the fifth grade in detention. He tied up weaker boys and threatened to burn them with a cigarette lighter. He grabbed girls behind the bleachers and forced them to pull their skirts up and their panties down. He made other kids give him their lunch money and threatened to kill them if they told their parents. Eventually most everyone in town heard about Mack, and what they learned scared them. More than one closed-door PTA meeting was convened to discuss this fifth-grade teenager who belonged in a different kind of school — reform school. People said it would happen before long, and they were right.

The last straw came when Mack went to the principal's office for groping his teacher after class. He called Mack's grandparents, and it surprised him when the boy's grandmother actually showed up. His guardians had never shown any interest in Mack, but for some reason, she came this time. He outlined the problems Mack created, and he was just getting to his recommendation that the man-child be sent somewhere for counseling when Mack flew across the desk and grabbed the principal by his tie. While his grandmother watched helplessly, Mack stuck his fist into the man's face and screamed, "I'll kill you, you bastard! You won't do anything to me because I'll come after you and your family!"

That marked the end of Mack's formal education, such as it had been. He was expelled, and a restraining order kept him off the school grounds. The principal filed a formal complaint, child services workers came down from the parish seat in New Iberia, and Mack's grandparents were given two choices. They could voluntarily surrender him to juvenile authorities or face a guardianship termination hearing. Either way, Mack was going to reform school.

The decision was an easy one. They hadn't wanted Mack in the first place, and the more dangerous and belligerent he became, the more afraid of him they were. They had had enough, and they requested a termination hearing, explaining to the judge that they were too old to keep him. The magistrate agreed and freed the old couple from the boy they firmly believed was destined for a life behind bars, or worse.

At age fifteen, Mack entered the Louisiana criminal system for the first time. With a fifth-grade education and an attitude, he was sentenced to three years at the Barksdale Juvenile Detention Center, a place with a reputation for being hell on earth for bad boys. Instead of rehabilitation and education to transform delinquents into productive citizens, inmates as young as twelve and as old as twenty lived together in dormitories. Too much idle time resulted in fights and an occasional murder. Uneducated, underpaid guards routinely baited the boys, placing bets on who would win barefisted boxing matches that sometimes sent participants to the prison hospital.

The warden — a corpulent man who nipped at a bottle of Old Crow in his desk drawer during the day — could not have cared less who got hurt. A few years ago, he'd been an administrator at Angola. That ended when he was caught bringing drugs into the prison to sell to inmates. Afraid of repercussions from the state capitol, the prison board kept things quiet and moved their lawbreaking employee to Barksdale to run the reform school. It was a recipe for disaster, and disaster was the best word to describe the warden's tenure. Barksdale was horrible. The youthful offenders who finished their sentences inevitably graduated to major crimes, relying upon the friendships they'd made in reform school and the street skills they'd learned to build careers as drug dealers, thieves, rapists and murderers.

Mack Thorn fit in perfectly. At Barksdale he met Samuel Gold, a boy his age from his home parish and strong and husky like Mack. Sam was there for molesting two young male cousins. Like Mack, he would be there until his majority at eighteen. After half-hearted attempts to bully Sam, Mack joined forces with him, and they extorted whatever favors or money they wanted from the others. Inmates and guards alike stayed away from them, and the two literally ran Barksdale until their release. They never expected to see each other again.

Mack went back home broke, jobless, and with a massive chip on his shoulder against the world in general and his grandparents in particular. In his twisted mind, he blamed them for sending him off to reform school. He tried and failed to find work. Everyone knew Mack, and nobody would take a chance on that bizarre kid. He had to leave town to find work, so he stole his grandfather's car, drove from place to place, and finally landed a job working on a pig farm outside St. Martinville. That lasted for a few months until Mack assaulted the daughter of the farm's owner. Her father knew Mack had a violent streak, and he wouldn't let his daughter testify. Mack lost his job, one he told himself he hadn't wanted in the first place, but that was all.

His grandfather demanded the car back, and Mack taught him a little lesson about making demands he couldn't back up. The old man ended up in the hospital, but once again Mack walked away free, because his grandparents wouldn't press charges either. After that he left town and went to Lafayette, a city where nobody knew him. He got a job with a man who felt sorry for this giant of a kid who didn't know proper English, seemed moody and sullen, and needed a break.

Mack's new job was on the back of a garbage truck doing weekly rural trash pickups. He made more money than he'd ever seen before — a hundred and fifty dollars a week — and the work was easy. As the crew made rounds, Mack cased the houses on his route. He learned who stayed home in the day and who didn't, who had dogs, and who left things on the front porch that he could steal.

Tall and muscular, he could pass for someone much older than eighteen, and he used a fake ID to buy beer every night after work. In a bar he met a waitress his age named Susanna, who became enamored at his worldliness and ended up both in love and pregnant. She talked Mack into marrying her, and for a few months it seemed Mack's life had taken a new, positive direction. But one night in a fit of rage over nothing, Mack beat his pregnant wife. Their daughter was stillborn. He blamed her for the death and hit her some more. From then on, she cowered in fear every time he came home from work.

Mack's marriage didn't change him much. As he rode the truck, he saw a teenaged girl hanging laundry on a clothesline in her yard. He began watching her house at night, hoping she'd come outside.

When she finally did, he grabbed her, clamped his hand over her mouth, and dragged her into a field next door. He assaulted her, promised to kill her if she told anyone, and then he disappeared into the night. The girl didn't talk, so he did it to someone else a month later. That girl reported the crime, but she had no idea who the assailant was, so nothing happened to Mack.

The third time, things went badly. He broke a window and climbed into the bedroom of an eighteen-year-old he'd had his eye on. The girl pepper-sprayed him and kneed him in the groin, so he punched her over and over until she was still, and he finished what he'd come for. When he stood and zipped up, he noticed she wasn't moving, but he didn't care. He'd gotten what he wanted, but this time he got far more than he bargained for. The girl was dead.

He pushed the body through the window, drove her down to a remote part of the Bayou Teche, and used a hatchet to dismember her corpse, leaving the parts in a clump of bushes on the shoreline. A month or so later some fishermen wondered what was causing the awful stench, and to their horror, they soon found out. There was enough to identify her and establish that she'd been raped and murdered.

Investigators connected some apparently random events. Several crimes had occurred on one rural trash route, and they interrogated the men who worked the truck. Mack never had lied well, and his alibi was full of holes. At his trial, he narrowly escaped the death penalty. He was sentenced to life in prison at the maximum-security facility in Angola, Louisiana. Mack was already a criminal. Now, at age twenty-two, he was in for life.

Four years later, two old friends met in the prison yard, and it was hard to tell who was more surprised. Mack and Sam slapped each other on the back, shared a cigarette, and caught up on what they'd been doing since reform school. The former juvenile delinquents had become dangerous, hardened criminals. They were very similar in one respect — they were both so mentally off-kilter that basic rules of society meant nothing to them.

Like Mack, Sam was a brutally violent man. After his release from Barksdale, he'd moved back to the family farm in rural Iberia Parish. He started carrying a gun everywhere he went, and he spent the night in jail now and then for brandishing it in public places, usually when he was on one of his frequent drunken binges. One sunny afternoon he stopped into a fast-food burger joint, pushed to the head of the line, and ordered a sandwich. The people behind him complained, and one unfortunate soul gave Sam a good shove.

Sam took out his pistol, killed everyone in line, and — simply because it seemed like a reasonable thing to do — he shot the clerk behind the counter. Then he sat down in a booth, laid his gun on the table, ate his burger until the police arrived, and surrendered without incident.

After a brief trial, Sam's attorney stated in his closing argument that his client was insane and incapable of knowing the difference between right and wrong. A psychiatrist had testified as much, but this jury had no intention of letting him go free. This psychopath wasn't going to a mental hospital for a few years, just to get out and do it all over again. Samuel Gold needed to be removed from the population. Permanently.

Unlike some Southern states, Louisiana executed prisoners rarely, the last having been over seven years earlier. So the jury gave him five life sentences, one for each of the people he'd gunned down. The judge ruled he must serve them consecutively, without the chance for parole. Sam would never be free again, or at least that was the intention.

Mack had been at Angola a year when his old friend arrived. He'd been sent to the Hole — solitary confinement — a few times for fighting. He got crazy when he was angry, and inmates started calling him Mad Mack, just like his grade school classmates had. Even longtimers in the maximum-security penitentiary knew to be careful of the crazy ones, and they figured out quickly that Mack was a total lunatic. Most people steered clear of Mack when he was out in the prison yard. The ones who didn't ended up in the hospital.

In many prisons, men like Mack and Sam — unstable, prone-to-violence inmates serving long sentences for heinous crimes — wouldn't have been allowed to mingle with others. At Angola, the warden hoped to keep the population calm by affording them this minor privilege. No one had escaped from this fortress in years, so the only issue with putting the men together was that people died now and then. The warden thought to himself that there was a positive side — every death reduced the overcrowded population.

Sam was the only friend Mack had, and surprisingly, there was never any problem between them. Mack joined the Aryan Brotherhood, a savage prison gang whose activities fit his personality perfectly. Sam joined too, and as a team they carried out thefts, extortion and other crimes against the population. Despite all that, Sam somehow managed to stay out of the Hole, but Mad Mack's mouth and his fists put him there more and more often as the months went by. When he'd cuss out a guard or pummel another inmate half to death, the guards would beat him with batons, and Sam wouldn't see his friend for a month. One day Mack would walk out in the yard, squinting his eyes against the sun he hadn't seen for days, and itching to fight anybody who crossed him.

A friend of Sam's from back home — a man in his twenties named Thomas Small — appeared in the prison yard one afternoon. Mack met him, and before long their twosome became three. Tom was a vicious rapist who was in his first month of a forty-year sentence. A slim and frail man, he was glad to be under Mad Mack's protection and free from the intimidation and brutal treatment dished out to "fresh meat" — new inmates like himself.

The three spent hours every day together, and eventually they collaborated on a plan to escape. With little to lose and everything to gain, it made perfect sense to them. If they were caught, what was the worst thing that could happen? They'd go to the Hole.

"It ain't that bad," Mad Mack would say with a wink. "If you like bread and water and being in the dark all the time, you're gonna love it!"

They worked, they patiently waited, and they violently silenced anyone who asked questions about what they were doing. They dug a tunnel, and when they were finished, they concealed it carefully. After that the waiting got harder, because now they were ready.

"Stay cool," Mack told the others. "Everything's got to be right. I'll tell you when."

CHAPTER NINE

In the days before Mack got expelled and sent to reform school, back when he was a muscular teenager repeating the fifth grade, he would entice his three-year-younger classmates into going with him for an adventure. An invitation from Mack flattered them — he was a curiosity, he was older, and they looked up to him as younger kids often do. They didn't know what he had in mind when he took them to the abandoned prison in Victory.

One afternoon, he led a classmate through the darkened entryway into the large front room. Plaster from the ceiling covered the floor with a white powder. Boards had fallen too, and rats scurried from their nests.

"Where are we?" the young boy asked. His voice trembled, and Mack smiled. He wove a tale guaranteed to terrify his younger companion.

"This is the Victory Institution for the Criminally Insane. They kept the very worst prisoners here. They locked them up and chained them to the walls. The doctors did experiments on them, transplants and stuff without even knocking them out, to see if they could stand the pain. People could hear the screams all the way into town, and that's half a mile away!"

Mack dragged the terrified boy along a hallway and pointed to rooms with bars over the windows. "See those cells? That's where they'd beat the inmates with whips just for fun."

His face white with fear, the boy listened to Mack's stories. Every kid knew about this place; the building was almost two hundred years old, and it really had been a penitentiary for the worst offenders. There also were ghosts, people said. That made the little kid even more frightened because he didn't know if Mack's story was the truth or made-up.

"Want to see where they killed the prisoners?" He laughed as the boy shook his head and backed away. "Oh, come on. Don't be a sissy!" He made the kid go into a tiny room with him.

Over the past couple of years, Mack had explored every square inch of this creepy old building, and he always brought the younger boys to this room. This place scared his classmates the most, because of something Mack had found. There was a false wall, and when he touched a trip mechanism, the wall would slowly swing open to reveal a hidden stairway leading down into the blackness. It was something straight out of a movie, and it was guaranteed to terrify his young companions.

"The torture chamber's down there. Come on! I'll show you!"

Tears streaming down his face, the boy jerked his arm away. "No, Mack! I'm not going! I want to go home!"

Like all the others, this one ran for his life, stumbling through the debris in the entryway and running out into the sunlight. Mack figured he'd cry all the way home, and that made him laugh out loud. None of the boys had gone downstairs; if they had, they'd have seen that it was nothing but an empty room beneath the ground.

In reality, there was something interesting about the room. He'd discovered a tunnel that led to a real dungeon — cells and all — but he'd never show that to anyone. It was his secret place. He'd even built a hideout in another room off the main chamber.

Every time he came here alone, he brought stuff — old furniture, nonperishables, and things he found or stole that would make his secret room comfortable. To normal kids, this hideout might have been a place to play or sneak a smoke, or a clubhouse that required a password to enter. Mack's mind didn't work that way. He built his underground sanctuary so he could escape someday. Not escape as in get away, but escape as in hide. From whom, he didn't know yet. But he was sure it was going to happen sometime, and that excited him.

CHAPTER TEN

Mack had come a long way. As a teenager, he'd brought kids to the Asylum and scared them with tales of an underground torture chamber. Now, as an adult, he lived down there himself. It made him smile to think how long he'd kept this place a secret.

The dinner dishes sat neatly on the kitchen table, all dried, stacked and ready for breakfast. Mack whistled softly as he straightened his chair, used a rag to wipe the tabletop, and put the silverware he'd washed in a canister. Although there were two of them, Mack ended up doing all the work around the house. He liked it that way. He wanted things just so, and Sam didn't much care about anything. After all these years, he did everything himself.

He glanced at Sam and said, "You didn't touch your dinner. Why do you keep worrying about things?" Sam sat where he always sat, in the old recliner Mack had found somewhere and hauled through the passageway into the large single room that served as their kitchen, bedroom and living area. "You need to quit fretting about everything and be positive for a change!"

Mack paused, cocked his head and listened, and said, "Sam, I swear the older you get, the more crazy your thoughts are. Don't you understand that they forgot about us a long time ago? I've told you that a thousand times. Can't you get that through your thick skull?" He shook his head and brewed a cup of tea on the Coleman camp stove. He didn't ask Sam because he never wanted a cup.

"We're almost out of propane," Mack said. "Want to go get some, or shall I?" He laughed at the joke — Sam hadn't done anything productive in years. He just sat in that chair and sulked all day. Mack was used to it by now. Hell, how long had it been? Thirty years? That realization made Mack raise his eyebrows in surprise. *Time flies when you're getting old*, he thought to himself.

He walked down a passage, climbed a ladder, popped a cover, and stepped out into a thick grove of trees. Moonbeams pierced the canopy high above. He walked to where the woods ended, moved some brush, and pulled back an old camouflage tarp he'd found a long time ago. He stepped out into the field and looked both ways to be sure he was alone. He got on the motorcycle that had been under the tarp, started it up and drove eight miles down Highway 182. Some nights he'd go the other direction, heading to Charenton or Glencoe. He never picked the same town twice in a month so as not to attract unnecessary attention. A few things missing here and there wouldn't even warrant a call to the sheriff, as long as he was careful and didn't hit the same place twice.

This late, every store in the little town was dark. As he passed houses on the main avenue, he could see the flickers of TVs in living rooms, wives cleaning up after supper, and he could almost feel the warmth and smells of family, togetherness and home-cooked meals. He shook his head to dismiss those crazy thoughts. He hadn't ever known family or warmth, and now he lived his life the way he wanted to. He was on his own and accountable to nobody.

He cut the motor and coasted in to the Dollar General store on the south end of town. He saw one dim streetlight a hundred yards away and no security cameras outside the building. He'd checked this place out a while back, like he had a hundred others, entering each one into his notebook for future reference. The notation for this store said "propane," and that was what Mack needed tonight.

On the side of the building, there was one of those wire cage setups that held propane tanks. Some of the flimsy locks were broken — two more wouldn't attract any attention. As usual, several empty canisters sat on the ground where people had returned them. The instructions clearly said to put your empty one in the cage when you removed the new one, and it made Mack mad that the shiftless jerks threw them on the ground. Even though their laziness was a break for him, it still irritated him.

He took an all-purpose tool from his pocket, snapped the locks on two cages and removed full propane bottles, replacing them with the discarded ones. He used a piece of wire to close the cage doors, and everything looked like it had before he came. It might be days before anyone noticed what he'd done. Dollar General didn't care if something was missing — the propane company ate the loss. Nobody ever called the cops; stealing a tank of propane just wasn't a big deal.

He secured the canisters onto the back of his cycle, one on each side, and rode off into the night. He'd done this same thing so many times it was a breeze. Whatever he needed, he set out and stole it. People might wonder about little things that disappeared, but they didn't give it much thought. Things would have been different if they knew a vicious murderer was the culprit.

Years had passed since Mack's escape. As he aged and grew a beard, he began to venture out now and then. Soon he felt comfortable in public places. He was careful. Even though everyone around here thought he was dead, he didn't want anyone thinking they recognized him.

After a while, he would ride to nearby towns and do things others took for granted — being outdoors, window-shopping in the bright sunshine, saying good morning to strangers he met. He might be a disturbed man capable of heinous acts, but Mack had been lonely. He didn't like people, but he liked doing things normal people did.

A few of the newest flat-screen TVs were in a store window he passed, and he went inside to check them out. He wouldn't have one himself — in his and Sam's situation, it made no sense, and he hadn't watched TV in years. He wanted to see the latest technology. Like they do in stores, the sets were all tuned to the same channel and there was no sound. He saw a rerun of *Sixty Minutes* and was interested in the segment that was running. There were only two customers in the place, and neither was looking his way, so he turned up the volume slightly.

He watched a news guy interviewing a man dressed in a fine pinstriped suit with a starched white shirt and flashy gold cufflinks. His red tie and pocket handkerchief were more signs that this was a successful leader, a powerful man respected by others. The news guys called him a fraud and a huckster, but Mack admired his ingenuity. And what the guy was doing gave Mack an idea. He needed a change in his life, and he began to think how he might make it happen.

CHAPTER ELEVEN

The clock showed 1:53 a.m. Landry was halfway through his nine-hour graveyard shift in the sheriff's office. He muted the television once the fourth episode of *I Love Lucy* started. He could stand only so much of Lucy's repetitive foolishness. The only sounds came from two drunks snoring back in the jail.

At two a.m., the deputies patrolling the parish checked in. If this night was typical, things would be dead until three. Landry turned to the computer, brought up the database that his boss ordered him to stay out of, and started his search.

Something was missing, and this time he concentrated only on the thirteen deaths since 1989. He read every entry for each case and wrote detailed information on the pad where he kept his notes.

The first unsolved murder occurred on June 10, 1989, a woman five feet four and around twenty years old. The autopsy report showed a variety of illegal drugs in her system. She had marks and bruises everywhere on her ninety-five-pound naked, emaciated body. She was struck in the head with a blunt instrument, maybe a pipe or a bat, that fractured her skull. She died instantly and had been raped posthumously. No one knew her name, why she died or who killed her.

He thought it might be interesting to check the databases from nearby rural parishes the same size as Iberia's. Did they too have unsolved murders every so often? That was a project for another night.

His yellow pad overflowed with information as he came to the most recent deaths, the three fraternity boys found in the early morning of June 11, 2012. When he finished, he studied the notes to see if there was a link among these seemingly unrelated cases.

He now saw something he'd missed earlier — the remarkable similarity in the dates. All thirteen deaths had happened in June. In the fraternity incident, the coroner had estimated the time of death at 11:30 p.m. June 10 for the boy who was hanged. The others had died the next morning, after their friends had returned for them.

The dates of death for the others — homeless people who sought shelter in the abandoned building — were harder to pinpoint because some had been found soon after death while others had been in the house for weeks, the longest being a body discovered on July 9, 2004. The coroner had estimated that person had died a month earlier — in June, like the rest.

The dates might easily be wrong. His estimates might be off by days, but every single murder had happened in June, and almost every one *could* have occurred on the tenth of June. There was something significant about that date. That enigma deserved more investigation.

He altered his search terms, looking for every unsolved crime in Iberia Parish that had occurred on June 10. He found one — a gruesome double murder. Landry pulled up that case.

On June 10, 1991, someone had murdered two people asleep in their townhouse in an affluent suburb of New Iberia. The perpetrator had entered through an unlocked garage door and savagely attacked the couple, a prominent attorney named James Christian Romero and his wife Susanna. Like the ones at the Asylum, this case was still unsolved twenty-seven years later.

Were these murders related to the ones twenty miles away in Victory? They had occurred more than a year before Landry's birth, but he'd never heard of them, and that surprised him, as gruesome as they were.

There was a link to an article in the local newspaper, but Landry needed a subscription to view the story. He jotted down the relevant facts and decided he'd visit the newspaper office on his next day off. If thirteen murders at the Asylum — and now an apparently unrelated one — had happened on the same day, and there were no other unsolved murders on any other days in this parish since 1989, how could it all be a coincidence? Maybe the murders of the lawyer and his wife had nothing to do with the Asylum, but the date alone merited further investigation.

A few days later Landry went to the *Daily Iberian* newspaper and asked to view the archives for information about a murder in June 1991. A clerk escorted him to a cubicle where an ancient microfiche reader sat on a desk, and went off to retrieve the records Landry had requested. After a quick lesson on the machine, Landry scrolled through the editions of the *Daily Iberian* for the days after the murder.

The issue for June 11 had two enormous black words as the lead headline — "DOUBLE MURDER." The story filled the top half of the front page and included a picture of the crime scene, an attractive home in a gated community. The crime occurred sometime during the night of June tenth or the early morning of the eleventh. The police department's public information officer issued a statement assuring the public that the crime would be solved quickly. But in another story on the same page, the chief of police stated that they had few clues so far.

Over the next two weeks there were more articles. At first there was optimism, with calls for citizens to report anything suspicious. A ten-thousand-dollar reward escalated to twenty-five, then fifty, but nothing seemed to help. By the end of June — twenty days after the double murders — a citizens' group filled the city council chamber and demanded Chief Cormier be fired. The leader of that group, a prominent merchant, said the town still lived in fear almost three weeks after the slayings. People barricaded themselves in their homes, stayed inside after dark, and the sales of handguns and rifles had increased three hundred percent over the previous month.

The spokesman read from a prepared statement he also gave to a reporter in the room. "Except for the gun shops, local merchants are suffering because of Chief Cormier's lack of action. Our citizens are living in fear, and it's up to the council to do something."

Wondering what had happened, Landry scrolled through the issues for every day in July. The council didn't take action — there was no story about the chief's firing — and people returned to normal lives as the days and weeks passed.

An article on July 24 included the coroner's report. The attorney's throat had been savagely slashed. His wife, Susanna's body had been dismembered, most likely with a hatchet. There were no murder weapons on the scene, no fingerprints, and no other clues about the killer or killers. The crimes remained unsolved and open.

On October 31, Chief Cormier resigned to become chief of police in Madison, Mississippi, a town with a police force similar in size to New Iberia's. The city council elevated the assistant chief to the position, and he gave a statement to the press, saying his primary goal would be to solve the murders of James and Susanna Romero. Landry read the words years later and knew that goal still hadn't been realized.

There was no mention of any other crimes on or around June 10 in the years before or afterwards. Nor did anyone make the simple connection Landry had made — that every remaining unsolved murder in Iberia Parish since 1989 had happened on or near the same day.

The stories petered out after a while. He scrolled down to the first anniversary of the slayings — June 10, 1992, and he found another front-page article with the headline "STILL UNSOLVED" and a year-old photo of two corpses covered with sheets at the morgue. There was an interview with the mayor, two members of the city council, and the merchant who had led the citizens' coalition that addressed the council a year ago.

The consensus was that although the murders had grown cold, all it would take was one break — one crucial tip from someone in the know — to wrap up this case and bring the perpetrators to justice. The tone of the article was as upbeat as the city leaders could spin it. Crime was down overall, nothing else had happened in twelve months, and life was good in the heart of Cajun country. Tourists were coming in record numbers. From Landry's perspective, the attitude of everyone seemed to be that it was best to let sleeping dogs lie.

BILL THOMPSON

And those particular dogs had lain for almost twenty-seven years.

CHAPTER TWELVE

Landry was sure there was something he could learn from all this information, but he was lost. Every time he had office duty, he tweaked his list, looking for anything — similarities, links, any little clue he might have missed. One night he wrote down every year that had a cold case. Beginning in 1989, there had been eleven crimes and thirteen victims. The last incident was the deaths of the three fraternity pledges in 2012.

Landry was convinced that there was a single perpetrator. When there were others, someone always talked, but this man had kept the secret. He had murdered people in eleven of the past twenty-eight years, twelve if you counted the lawyer and his wife. In the other seventeen years, there were no violent crimes.

Is that right? I'm missing something. What am I missing?

He looked at the data again. Every case was listed. There were no unsolved cases in the other years.

Then it came to him. He was only seeing part of the picture — the cold cases — because he was only searching for *unsolved* crimes. He did a new search, looking for *every* crime in the parish since 1980 that happened around June 10. There were hundreds of them — car thefts, burglaries, drug offenses, assaults, domestic violence issues, a kidnapping involving a custody dispute, and many minor offenses. Each had disrupted someone's life to a greater or lesser degree, but now they were just line items on a spreadsheet — statistics that ended up in an annual report to the state.

He sorted and filtered, trying to see what data would give him a broader view. At last his search was so narrow that something turned up. Last year on June 10, a female in her twenties died from a stabbing in the prison cemetery behind the main building. There was a second body inside the Asylum — a man roughly the same age as the victim who had overdosed on heroin. A pipe and residue from the drug lay next to him, and his bloody hands held the knife that was the murder weapon. Their clothes, blankets and personal things were strewn about him. Investigators concluded the two were homeless and had been staying at the Asylum for days, maybe weeks. He killed her outdoors, went back to the building and overdosed.

Slam bam, case closed. On to the next one. This case was neatly tied up, the bodies were sent to their parents, and two middle-class families wept over the senseless deaths of two young addicts.

Since this incident was recent, Landry could access reports from the investigation, the autopsy report and the coroner's determination of death. He read everything and wondered if the state police had been correct. According to them, the evidence clearly showed how the girl died and who killed her, and that was that. Landry also knew the cops needed to solve crimes instead of expanding the unsolved cases list.

Even though he had no training in crime scene investigation, Landry began second-guessing the experts. Their conclusion was simple, as if someone wanted to close a case that didn't deserve further effort. They were two young trespassers thousands of miles from home, squatting in an old building.

Landry didn't consider this a murder-suicide at all. They had wandered into a strange place where unexplained murders had occurred over and over, and they picked June tenth, the wrong day to spend the night at the Asylum. Was the pair aware of the building's past? Probably not. Whether they had arrived together or separately, the two had chosen that place out of convenience, and both had ended up dead for having done so.

Something in his gut told Landry there was more to this case. He tried to shrug it off, telling himself he'd spent so much time examining the others, he was skeptical of everything. But he couldn't dismiss the obvious questions and inconsistencies. The girl's body lay in a prison cemetery half a mile from the house — a place Cate had told him about. If the police report was correct, the man killed the girl with a knife in the cemetery, went back to the main structure, sat down on the floor and, holding the murder weapon in his bloody hands, he overdosed.

It couldn't have happened like that. This case belonged in the "unsolved mysteries" file with the others. He was beginning to see that the same person had committed all the crimes since 1989. They were similar, and this one fit the pattern. The murder weapon, a knife, had been used in other murders. Finding a body in the cemetery was a first — the others were killed inside the building or close by — but it didn't change things. Maybe the killer murdered both of them inside and then he took her body to the cemetery. He put the knife in her friend's hand, spread her blood around and created a simple connect-the-dots for authorities to identify the wrong murderer.

He was sure their case belonged on his list. Another June 10 murder conveniently solved, but actually still open.

At six a.m. Landry's shift was almost over, and he struggled to stay alert for his last hour. He must have fallen asleep for a moment, because his head snapped up when the office door opened and the sheriff walked in two hours earlier than usual. The boss stopped at Landry's desk, asked if everything had been quiet, and said he had a meeting in Baton Rouge that morning. He'd stopped by the office to get his briefcase before hitting the road.

He picked up the thick legal pad filled with Landry's notes. "What's this?"

"It's … it's just something I'm doing to pass the time. I think it's interesting to look up old cases in the database, that's all."

"This is about the cold cases, isn't it? You just can't let it go. I told you that state police cases aren't our concern. But you've got a list going — you're planning to tackle them yourself, even though you know as much about investigating as my dog does. Listen to me and listen good, Landry. I've half a mind to put a reprimand in your personnel file and fire you on the spot for failing to follow an order. If I did that, you'd never get another job in law enforcement anywhere, not that you care about that. I'm giving you a break this time. But this is the last time. You disobey me again and you're out of here. Do you understand?"

Landry nodded. "I found something —"

"Dammit, boy! Are you gonna force me to fire you? I asked you if you understood this was the last time. So answer me!"

84

"I understand, Sheriff. It won't happen again."

And with that, Landry's boss stormed into his office and slammed the door, taking Landry's legal pad with him.

At seven, the day-shift guys came in and relieved Landry. The sheriff was still in his office with the door closed. For a moment, Landry had thought about going in there and taking the pad if his boss left before he did, but that was crazy, and it would cost him his job. Better to wait and figure something out.

It had taken many hours to build that list. He'd looked at every case for the past forty years and selected the eleven — now twelve — that he believed were related. If he couldn't get that pad out of the sheriff's office, he'd have to start from the beginning. There must be a way to get his notes back.

CHAPTER THIRTEEN

A run-down four-room log cabin sat in a thick grove of trees on a tiny island in the middle of Bayou Teche. Except for dense foliage along the riverbank, a person standing on the island's rocky shore could have seen the old prison. The Asylum was less than half a mile away.

Back in the 1990s, Hank Pitfield bought the island for a few thousand dollars and built his retreat. Hank was the most famous football player ever to come out of Iberia Parish. He was a star at the University of Florida, and then the Steelers drafted him. The New Orleans Saints picked up Hank in the late eighties, and he was glad to come back home and play for his favorite team.

He was dead and gone now, but his cabin still stood in the center of the island, surrounded by trees and brush. Hank had built it as a secret getaway — a retreat where he and his friends partied for days at a time, far away from fans and the media. He'd bought the place through a corporation so no one could trace it to him and intrude on his relaxation.

Hank was one of the Saints' star players, such as it was for a team that didn't win many games. They paid Hank a lot of money, and he played well. A pro football player had free time during the off-season, and he spent some of his down on the bayou. In that little cabin there had been prime steaks, top-shelf booze, Cuban cigars, and girls — lots of beautiful, high-priced women brought in by boat for a few days of whatever struck the guys' fancy.

A sign still hung above the front door, its faded letters in desperate need of a paint job like the rest of the place, but the words were decipherable. *Welcome to Lafitte Landing.* Hank had chosen the name because of the rumors. It had happened one spring weekend when he invited friends from New Orleans. One of his guests had told an interesting story about a legend called the Treasure of Bayou Teche.

It was a fact that there had been pirate activity in the area two hundred years ago. According to the legend, one of the buccaneers — Jean Lafitte by name — came upriver from the Gulf in a small boat. Six men — or maybe four or eight — buried the treasure on an uninhabited island in Bayou Teche. This could be that island, the guy from New Orleans said as they all sat around the poker table. The men all had a good laugh and gave Hank a hard time when he told them they were nuts. They said he'd be sorry if someone else found it first.

Did Hank look for the treasure before he died? No one knew the answer.

Every few years the media resurrected the story about pirate loot buried somewhere along the bayou. Every time it was shown, certain people — ones with an appetite for adventure — got caught up in the excitement all over again. One of those would-be treasure hunters was Michael, an IT specialist from Lafayette. Every night before bedtime,

Michael had story hour with his boys, Nixon and Tripp, who were both under ten. One night he spun a yarn about a buried chest full of gold, and his excited sons begged to go searching for it. The story arose from a legend Michael had heard from his own father, and as the eager boys talked about treasure, Michael decided to make it a boys' day out. Hunting for pirate loot would be fun.

One warm Saturday morning, Michael rented a small bass boat at the dock in New Iberia. He could have started farther south in Jeanerette, a couple of miles from his destination, but he wanted Nixon and Tripp to experience the river. The kids pointed out things as they puttered lazily along the scenic bayou through farms, a few housing developments, and dense forests that blocked the sunlight. A dozen kinds of angry birds cawed at them for breaking the reverie, and they saw a six-foot gator partly submerged in the water.

Today's journey was a twenty-two-mile round trip to Lafitte Landing. Even though treasure was all the boys could talk about, this was a father-son outing, a chance for more bonding while traveling down a peaceful river in a motorboat, telling pirate stories and cracking jokes. They'd have lunch somewhere along the way — sandwiches Michael's wife, Brittany, had packed in a cooler with some sodas.

They stopped at a few islands along the way and tried out a metal detector he'd borrowed, but Michael only found remnants from picnickers like pull tabs and aluminum foil. By noon it was time to visit the one they'd been waiting for — the island that people said Jean Lafitte had visited.

Although Hank tried to keep his ownership a secret, everyone knew about Lafitte Landing. It was large for the bayou, maybe three acres total, and dense forest covered almost all of it. Hank had built a cabin, but Michael didn't know if it was still there. As they came to it, they saw *No Trespassing* signs along the shore. Michael decided there was no harm in looking around. He had two young treasure hunters. They'd come this far, and he wasn't going to deny them their fun.

Michael maneuvered the boat to shore, grabbed his metal detector and stepped onto the rocky beach. He stopped and pointed at a footprint in the mud.

"Someone's been here recently."

Nixon was worried. "Is he still here, Dad? What if he's a bad guy?"

His dad assured him there were no bad guys around here.

They walked along an overgrown path, dodging briars and brambles, low-hanging limbs, and thick patches of poison ivy. The forest was so dense that they could see only a few feet ahead, and it surprised them when the trees ended and they walked into a field. The cabin stood a hundred feet away, and it looked to be in good condition.

Michael held his finger to his lips and pointed to the dilapidated building. Sounds came from inside; someone was moving around in the cabin.

"Is that the guy who made the footprint in the mud?" Tripp whispered, gripping his dad's hand.

"Let's find out. We're here anyway, so all he can do is tell us to leave." Making no effort to be quiet, they walked onto the porch, and Michael knocked on the door.

The sounds stopped. There was nothing now except the chirping and whirring of birds and insects around them.

"Hello? Is anybody home?"

Silence.

Michael stepped forward and turned the doorknob. To his surprise, the door swung open. He told the boys to stay on the porch and he stepped inside. When his eyes adjusted to the half-darkness, something startled him. He jumped backwards onto the porch and almost ran into his kids.

Scared, Tripp said, "What is it, Dad?"

"There's a guy in there with a shotgun! Let's get out of here!"

They turned to run, but a voice told them to stop. Michael obeyed. As they turned around, his kids started crying.

Michael drew them close. "It's okay," he whispered. "He won't hurt us. He wants to know who we are. That's all."

A tall, thin man stood on the porch, a shotgun cradled in his arms. He wore jeans and a flannel shirt, and his pencil-thin mustache reminded Michael of Rhett Butler in *Gone With the Wind*.

"What do you think you're doing?" he yelled, brandishing the weapon. "This is private property."

"Don't shoot us!" Nixon screamed.

"I'm sorry. We're taking a boat trip down the Teche and stopped here for lunch. We didn't even know if the cabin was still standing. Are you the owner?"

"Where are y'all from?"

"Lafayette. My name's Michael, and these are my boys, Nixon and Tripp. Sir, can you put down the gun? It's scaring the kids. We didn't mean to trespass —"

"You didn't mean to trespass?" the man roared. "Are you blind? There are signs everywhere." He pointed to the metal detector. "If you're just boating on the river, why did you bring that thing on my island? Planning on doing a little treasure hunting, are ya?"

Michael answered in a calm, respectful tone. His boys were holding onto his legs for dear life, and all he wanted now was to leave.

"I'm sorry we came on your property. We ... uh, like everyone, we've heard about the Treasure of Bayou Teche. We decided to go downriver from New Iberia and explore the islands. We've been to a few already."

"And you came on this one even though a dozen signs warned you not to. You're lucky I didn't shoot first. Get off my island or I'll call the sheriff and have you arrested."

"No, Dad!" Nixon screamed. "I don't want to go to jail!"

Michael backed away and said, "We're leaving, sir. I'm sorry, Mr. ... uh, I didn't get your name, sir."

"I didn't give it to you either. Get out of here before you make me mad!" He held the gun menacingly, gesturing with it for them to leave. The boys dragged their dad back to the shoreline. Within moments they were on the river. For a long time, the boys were quiet, which was unusual for these typically unrestrained kids.

At last Nixon whispered, "Dad, do you think that guy would have shot us?"

"No, son. There's no way. He didn't look like a bad guy. He was using his gun to scare us off his property, that's all. I heard that a doctor from Texas owns the island. Maybe that was him. That's all it was about. Don't worry about it anymore."

Despite Michael's reassuring words, their fun outing had ended when a gun-toting stranger terrified the kids. Michael drove the boat straight back to New Iberia, they ate sandwiches in the car, and by mid-afternoon Nixon and Tripp were back home safe and sound.

CHAPTER FOURTEEN

On a whim, Landry made another visit to the Iberia Parish Courthouse. He explained what he needed, and a clerk directed him to a PC where he could search the parish records. He'd met Cate Adams, and he looked forward to seeing her again, but right now he wanted to learn more about her father's hobby of buying properties at tax auctions. Did he own anything else around here?

Yes, he did, Landry soon discovered. He owned a lot — two hundred parcels in south Louisiana, and he'd bought each one for almost nothing. Landry's rough calculation showed he'd spent less than twenty thousand dollars total. Not an insignificant sum, but he was wealthy, and flipping just one property might recover the entire investment. The doctor's hobby impressed Landry. He was taking low-cost risks for potentially high rewards.

Madison John Adams bought his first properties in Louisiana in 2012, getting the Asylum and nineteen other parcels in one day. Two years later he bought forty more in a single day, including the three-acre island in Bayou Teche.

Landry knew about Hank Pitfield's island — everyone around here did — and he wondered how it ended up being auctioned for delinquent taxes. When Hank died, there was a bitter dispute between his divorced parents over his substantial estate. Some corporation Hank set up owned the island, and since his parents lived a thousand miles away, maybe they didn't realize it belonged to him. Whatever the reason it ended up in a tax sale, three acres and a cabin for a hundred bucks was a bargain.

Why did Cate's dad buy the island? Did he know the legend?

For centuries, locals had spun fanciful yarns about the islands. Every kid heard about pirate gold buried on an island in Bayou Teche near Jeanerette. The stories were believable because they contained an element of truth. There were pirates on the bayou in the eighteenth century. The problem was that dozens of islands dotted a hundred miles of rivers that wound through the countryside. Which island held the jackpot? People had searched for years, but nobody admitted finding anything. If they had, they kept it quiet.

Landry had heard the tales as a youth, but he didn't believe them. They were made-up fantasies to stimulate kids' imaginations and keep them occupied during long, sultry summers on the bayou. Some of his elementary school friends had gone on makeshift treasure hunts, but he didn't kill time that way. He'd rather fish away lazy summer afternoons.

Cate said her dad loved unexplained mysteries and the history of the Acadians. Did he pick up Hank's island because of the legend, or was Landry reading too much into his motives? Dr. Adams had bought properties sight unseen many times. This could be just another one.

Curious, he searched the web for the Treasure of Bayou Teche. More references and articles turned up than he'd expected, but he scrolled through most of them. If the title mentioned magic, aliens or time travel, Landry skipped it.

He saw what he termed "crackpot articles" — people who claimed they'd found the treasure but kept quiet so the government wouldn't take a share. If they were keeping so quiet, Landry mused, why did they reveal their discovery on the internet? He saw hand-drawn maps, requests for investors to join the hunt, and stories about Jean Lafitte's supposed visits to the area.

A few people said the legend had no factual basis. One author theorized that pirates came up Bayou Teche, but they left nothing behind. The river was a means to get to where they *really* intended to bury their loot, somewhere far away.

He found six articles worth printing; an archaeology professor at LSU wrote the most interesting one. The title — "Why I'm Certain the Treasure of Bayou Teche Exists" — got his attention. A scholar with a PhD believed the legend.

He debated asking Cate about the island, but decided against it. He'd only met her once, and he had no business asking why her dad bought properties. When he saw her again — if he saw her — maybe he'd ask.

He took the archaeologist's article with him on his rounds that night. Around two, he parked his patrol car on Parish Road 675 near Charlotte, turned on the dome light, read all thirty pages, and studied several maps. She described Lafitte's excursions into the area, but she gave lots of information he'd never heard before, and she provided solid evidence that pirate activity occurred in this part of Louisiana in the late 1700s.

The professor began with a familiar story, a factual account of buried treasure on Orange Island — now called

Jefferson Island. In the early 1900s, someone had unearthed old coins and a pirate's knife. Locals and the archaeologist herself believed they had been Lafitte's.

She presented evidence that the pirate had come to Bayou Teche. From extensive research and on-site visits, she concluded someone would find the treasure eventually, because it really was buried somewhere on the river.

The archaeologist's final sentence was intriguing. Landry considered it bold for a scientist; she obviously considered the legend true. "It remains for the diligent searcher — one can hope for an archaeologist with the training to preserve it — to unearth pirate booty left somewhere in what is now Iberia Parish by the pirate Jean Lafitte. In my professional opinion, discovering what Lafitte buried is not a matter of if, but when."

For the rest of his shift, Landry kept thinking about how confident the scholar was about the treasure. By the time he returned to the sheriff's office around six a.m., he had changed his mind about calling Cate. He wanted to know more. It wasn't his business, but if he explained how fascinating the story was, he hoped she'd give him more information.

He slept until mid-afternoon, ordered a pizza and gave her a ring, but she was busy and said she'd call back. He fidgeted, watched mindless television, and daydreamed about Jean Lafitte until the phone rang.

Cate wasn't aware her father owned an island, but added that there was nothing unusual about that. He owned hundreds of properties in several states. He didn't discuss the particulars of each one with her.

She was glad to hear that Landry was working on something less macabre than a series of unexplained deaths on the same night over three decades. Treasure-hunting might be a flight of fancy, but it sounded more upbeat than murder. She hadn't heard the Bayou Teche legend, but she promised to speak with her dad and let Landry know.

That evening he went to work; he was on office duty again tonight. Around midnight when everything was quiet, he made a bold decision. He had to get his notes back. There was something about the date of June 10 and the cold cases connected to it. He was certain he was close to an important breakthrough, and without his volume of notes, he had to start all over again.

Sheriff Barbour never locked his office door. Trembling, he stepped inside and flipped on the overhead light. If his boss showed up tonight for whatever reason, Landry's short career in law enforcement was history. Not once had the sheriff ever come here during the night shift, but if it happened tonight, that would be a disaster.

He hoped he might find the yellow pad somewhere on Sheriff Barbour's desk. He didn't see it; his boss kept a neat desktop — a pad that doubled as a monthly calendar, an old-fashioned Rolodex, the office phone, and a holder full of pens and pencils.

Dammit, now I have to open drawers!

Having gone this far, what difference did a little more burgling make? Sitting in the sheriff's chair, he opened first one drawer and then another. He saw personal things — a copy of *Hustler* magazine, a half-full pint bottle of bourbon, and a Valentine's card with lipstick kisses all over it from someone named Debbie — not Connie, his wife. But he didn't find his notes.

On a credenza behind him, Landry rifled through stacks of official reports, law enforcement journals and other work-related stuff, but what he wanted wasn't there.

He gave up, put things back, shut the door, and spent the last five hours of his shift searching the database and rebuilding his notes. When his replacement came in at 6:30, he put the notes in his backpack and headed home. He put his phone on do not disturb as usual and slept for several hours.

When he turned on his phone around 3:30, he saw he'd missed seven calls. Cate left a voicemail saying she had information, and to call when he could. He got goosebumps looking at the other six — all marked "unknown." That caller left no voicemails, but he didn't have to. The only unknown calls Landry ever got were from the Iberia County Sheriff's Office.

The sheriff was looking for him.

He debated for half an hour how he'd handle the situation and finally called to get it over with. The deputy who'd relieved him, a guy named Sean, answered.

"Shit, Landry! The sheriff's been trying to get hold of you all day! He's stormed in and out of his office a dozen times. He asked me why you didn't answer your phone, and I told him when we work nights, we turn off our phones when we're asleep. I thought he was going to send me over to your place, but about an hour ago he locked his office door and left."

He locked his office door. Landry knew he was busted, because the sheriff never did that.

"He's not there?"

"No, but he'll be back in twenty minutes. He told me if you called, I was to tell you to, in his exact words, get your ass down to the office as soon as possible."

"What does he want?"

"How should I know? When he first came in this morning, he was in his office with the door closed for almost an hour. Then the shitstorm started and he ranted about you not answering your phone. Are you coming in?"

"What choice do I have? Do you think I'm about to get fired?"

"I don't know. Did you do something? I just know I've never seen him this mad."

"Okay, I'll be there in twenty minutes."

"Good luck," Sean said. "From the looks of things around here, I think you're going to need it."

CHAPTER FIFTEEN

"Come on in, Landry," the sheriff said in a cordial voice. "Close that door behind you and take a chair."

Caught off guard by his boss's friendly demeanor after what Sean had prepared him for, Landry was cautious and wary. He sat across the desk from the sheriff, who leaned back in his chair, put his feet on the desk, and entwined his fingers behind his head. He pursed his lips a few times, and he didn't say anything for a very long time.

Landry broke the ice. "You, uh, you wanted to see me, sir?"

"Yes, son. Yes I did. How are things going?"

Landry's eyes widened a little, and the sheriff smirked.

"Uh, well, things are going just fine, I think. How do you think things are going?"

"Peachy. Just peachy. Anything going on in your life you want to talk about? Anything that might affect your work, that is?"

Where is he going with this? There had to be a connection between this conversation and Landry's activities during last night's shift; it was too coincidental otherwise. Until he found out, he had to be careful not to reveal something the sheriff didn't already know and make whatever this was a lot worse.

"Nothing comes to mind. All good, far as I'm concerned. I hope you think so too."

Sheriff Barbour seemed preoccupied. He leaned back in the chair while his eyes darted here and there all over the room. It made Landry uncomfortable, and he wondered again what the hell was going on.

At last the man spoke. "Have you ever heard of a product called Nest?"

"Nest?" Landry repeated. "No, sir. What is it?"

"A while back, the state gave all the parish sheriffs some money to upgrade security. You know all those lawsuits inmates file, claiming harassment, or they didn't get their porridge on time, or nobody read them a bedtime story? Stupid stuff like that. Well, the state found this product called Nest. It's a cheap security system that can record everything and make sure nobody can concoct a damn lie that wastes everybody's time and money."

Landry was desperately trying to be part of this conversation and to keep the sheriff calm. "I do recall somebody saying a few weeks ago that you were installing cameras in the jail."

"Yep, that's what we did. Had to be really careful, you know? Make sure they didn't accidentally get pictures of the pisser, know what I mean? Got to protect everybody's privacy these days. Even if you're a damned drunk or a car thief, you have rights. But sometimes those cameras are a good thing. They might help keep everyone out of trouble around here."

Landry was more confused than ever. "Sir, if this has something to do with my shift last night, I only went back into the jail when I was supposed to. Every hour on the hour I checked on the four guys back there. It's in the log."

Again the sheriff seemed not to hear him. He stared up at the ceiling and said, "We have a little tiny jail down here in Iberia Parish. Nothing as big as the ones up in Baton Rouge or even Lafayette. They sent us way too many cameras for our little tiny jail."

He stopped, and in one sudden move his feet came off the desk, his chair went upright, and he stared directly into Landry's eyes. "Know what I did with those other cameras?"

"No, sir."

"Take a look right there." He pointed to a small round white thing by the ceiling in the corner of his office. It had a tiny green light that glowed. "There's one of the little boogers we had left over. I put 'em all over the place. One in here, some out there in the office where you deputies work, pretty much everywhere but the bathrooms. They come in handy sometimes. Know what I mean?"

He glared across the desk, his face a distorted, angry red mass of blood vessels that looked like they were about to burst.

"I can explain, sir —"

The sheriff interrupted him. "And what can you explain, Deputy Drake? I haven't watched the video feed from last night, but I guess I should. I just wanted to see if you had anything to say when you found out you'd been on camera all night. And now it seems you do."

Shit! If he didn't watch the feed, what made him so mad all day? What does he know?

"I ... I may have fallen asleep once or twice on my shift, sir," Landry lied. "I was more tired than usual."

Barbour smiled. "I can certainly understand, son. It gets boring in here with nothing to do for nine hours straight. As long as you woke up when the deputies in the field reported in, no harm done."

"Yes, sir. And it only happened maybe twice."

"Well, good, then. That makes me feel better. Now, Landry. Let me throw out something else to you. Let's say I told you a little fib a minute ago. Let's say I did watch the footage from last night. Not all nine hours but some of it. If you knew that I watched video from your shift, would that change anything you have to tell me?"

"Uh, I'm not sure what you're getting at, Sheriff."

"What I'm *getting at*, Deputy Drake, is that you are in a buttload of trouble. You know what I saw. I want to hear it from you. Start talking."

"I came in here last night, sir. I worked for hours researching those cold cases, and I wanted to get my notes back so I could copy them. That's all I wanted, honest."

"So you went through every drawer in my desk and looked through my credenza, but you didn't find what you were looking for. Is that about it?"

"Yes, sir. That's what happened. I'm sorry —"

"Do you recall a conversation we had the other day when I came in early and caught you working on the cold cases? Do you remember what I told you?"

This was getting really bad really fast.

"Yes, sir."

"Why don't you refresh my memory?"

"Yes, sir. You said, uh, that I failed to follow an order, that you ought to fire me, and that you were giving me a break. But, sir, I'm onto something about those cases."

The sheriff interrupted him again. "And what was the last thing I told you that morning? What did I say I'd do if I caught you disobeying an order again?"

Landry hung his head. "You said you'd fire me, Sheriff. But please let me explain."

Barbour stood and leaned over his desk, towering over Landry, who appeared to be in shock. "Let *me* explain, son. You're so green that calling you a rookie isn't even fair. You haven't done jack shit since you got here except drive around the parish and sit in here all night every so often. Probation isn't even the word for where you stand in this office. You're the newest man on the force, yet you think you can run the show. You think you can go where you want, do what you wish. You can simply open old investigations, search the database, and suddenly you — the most brilliant crime solver since Eliot Ness — come up with astounding clues that even the state police overlooked.

"I gave you a direct order to stop working on those old cases. Last night you started it up all over again. You re-created the notes I took away from you. I saw you on the cameras. I looked at the video because I knew you couldn't let this go. You're too damned smart for your own good. You're fired. I'm withholding your pay for last night's shift, and I want your badge, pistol and all of our equipment back here on my desk in thirty minutes or I'll charge you with breaking and entering my office. Am I making myself clear, *Mister* Drake?"

"Yes, sir. I'm sorry, sir. I'll be back in thirty minutes."

Precisely twenty-two minutes later, Landry Drake was no longer a deputy sheriff. He was an unemployed person with less money in his bank account than it would take to pay his apartment rent twelve days from now. The quest for adventure and his zeal for discovering what was behind the

June tenth murders got in the way of common sense and obeying orders.

Landry went home, opened a beer, checked the stock of food in his refrigerator, decided he could live a few days on it, and sat in the dark until his phone rang. It was Cate, calling to find out why he hadn't returned her call from this morning. He had intended to tell her everything, but when she told him what she'd learned from her father, he forgot all about it.

CHAPTER SIXTEEN

Cate said she wanted to explain something before she told him what she'd learned. "I have this theory about Dad," she began. "The right side of his brain never grew up. He's an outstanding medical professional who lectures worldwide and is the smartest person I know. But his right brain — the daydreaming, imagining, wondering, outside-the-box part — drives him to believe in things like buried treasure and UFOs and ghosts and long-lost technologies. When I asked him about a legend called the Treasure of Bayou Teche, I saw the gleam in his eye. He smiled and asked if I'd been snooping around in his affairs. Not that he would care anyway, but he asked how I knew about the legend."

Landry smiled as she talked about her dad. He envied their close relationship, one he never had. His father worked two shifts, and on the rare occasions when he and Landry were awake at the same time, he was on his second or third beer of the day and in no mood to spend time with a kid.

He realized he'd been daydreaming, but he snapped back when she said, "I told him about you."

"Me?" That surprised him, although as close as she and her dad were, it shouldn't have. "What was there to tell?"

"He knew I went to the Asylum with you, and I told him you were researching unsolved mysteries out there. When you called yesterday, I told him you'd found out he owned a place called Lafitte Landing in Bayou Teche. He laughed and said you must be a detective, as good as you were at hunting down clues."

Right, Landry thought. *Not only am I not a detective, now I'm not even a deputy.* "Was he upset that I was nosing around his affairs?"

"Quite the opposite. Dad said you and he sounded alike, always wanting to know more about legends and mysteries. Then he told me about the island."

Cate's father explained that before bidding on these odd properties, he did an online search if he had time. Sometimes he turned up things — positive or negative — that influenced his decision. If a tiny, otherwise useless sliver of land ran alongside a highway or a shopping mall, it might be valuable to someone. But if another property was loaded with perpetual easements to some utility company so no one could build on it, then it was worthless. He'd bid on the first parcel and pass on the second.

Her father hadn't mentioned the island earlier because it wasn't important; he was buying parcels often, and this was one of two hundred he owned in south Louisiana alone. On the other hand, his purchase of the Asylum had been a big deal because he was fascinated by its history. He'd brought Cate and her mother there as a child. But this island wasn't anything special; it was just another of his tax auction properties. She confirmed, however, that he knew Hank Pitfield had owned the island, and he knew the treasure stories about Bayou Teche.

"So what did he say about the treasure?" Landry asked.

"He said he and I are coming over there to meet you and go to the island. We'll arrive Friday in time for dinner and go out Saturday. Does that work for you?"

At this point, he was available every single day and night, but now wasn't the time for that little revelation. "Damn right! What do you think he has in mind?"

"He said we're going on a treasure hunt!"

It was an exasperating four days for Landry, waiting for Friday to arrive. He searched the web for job openings in the area; there were more opportunities in Lafayette, since it was four times larger than New Iberia, but he hoped to stay in this area. It was nice to live where things moved a little more slowly, he saw people he knew every day, and — a critical component — apartments were cheaper.

He hoped that flipping burgers wasn't in his short-term future, but his financial situation was so dire that something had to happen fast. He had a full tank of gas and nowhere to go, so his immediate need was a couple of hundred dollars to bridge the gap between his bank balance and his upcoming rent payment.

There were dozens of jobs available that paid minimum wage, any of which he could have had with nothing more than a phone call. He was a college graduate, although his degree was worthless if he ended up as a route driver for Pepsi, a detail guy at a drive-through car wash, or a stocker at Safeway. The job searches made him realize what a screwup he'd been at the sheriff's office. It was his fault, and he'd have to take whatever he could find, even at eight or nine bucks an hour. He could always keep looking for that dream job.

Yeah, right. There's no dream job out there for me.

Landry made a decision and promised he'd stick to it. He'd go with Cate and her father this weekend, and Monday would be his deadline day. He'd either find something that he liked, or he'd take what was available.

He spoke with Cate on Thursday to ask what hotel they'd be in and when they would meet up. She laughed and said, "I thought you'd know my dad better than that by now. He's not much of a hotel person when he's in historical places like Cajun country. We're staying in a cottage at Rip Van Winkle Gardens on Jefferson Island. Have you heard of it?"

He had. The grande dame of the site was a beautiful house built in 1870 by a famous actor who played Rip Van Winkle on Broadway. It overlooked Lake Peigneur, and on the grounds were majestic trees, beautiful flowers and strutting peacocks. A few small cottages were available for overnight stays, and guests enjoyed the peaceful, serene atmosphere of the lake and the property.

"Have you been there before?"

"No. Dad chose it because he wants to tour the Joseph Jefferson house tomorrow afternoon before we meet you for dinner. We have reservations at seven at the restaurant on the property. We can have drinks and dinner and go over the plans for Saturday. Can you join us there?"

Yes, he could, and he told her he was looking forward to meeting her father.

He sat for several minutes after the call ended, hoping Cate's father would pick up the dinner check. Café Jefferson was an intimate, sophisticated restaurant with outside seating that looked over the scenic lake. It wouldn't be cheap, and if Landry somehow ended up with the bill, his debit card would never stand the strain.

Forcing positive thoughts into his head, he went to bed and thought of places he could apply for work that would at least be stimulating and interesting, even if the pay wasn't great. He began to craft a résumé in his mind. There wasn't much to say — there had only been college and the one job, one from which he'd been fired after only a few weeks. He had no idea what the sheriff would say if a prospective employer asked for a reference, but he was desperate. He'd been making nearly twenty dollars an hour. Now he was hoping for half that.

Landry awoke on Friday morning after a surprisingly good rest. He'd tossed and turned the other nights since his termination, but now that he had a plan, his mind stopped running ninety miles an hour and let him sleep. He had thought of one place to go today that might be a possibility for employment. He created a résumé on the computer, listed his job as deputy sheriff and his reason for leaving as "disagreement with a supervisor." He didn't know how he'd respond when someone asked what that meant.

He walked into the headquarters of the *Daily Iberian*, the local newspaper for the parish. The paper came out in the afternoon, and Landry knew that meant the mornings would be crazy with deadlines and work. Around noon the paper would be ready to print and the employees would begin working on tomorrow's edition, but the frenzy would be over for the day. He had chosen two p.m. to drop in, and he hoped the place was casual enough that he wouldn't need an appointment.

He was right. He was ushered to a cubicle where a sign read "Ty Jones, Editor." Inside, a man with long hair and horn-rimmed glasses sat behind a desk piled high with stacks of magazines, clippings, Post-it notes and everything else imaginable. There was a coffee cup in the middle of the mess. On Landry's side, lost in the clutter, there was a half-eaten hamburger in a Wendy's wrapper.

He stuck his hand across the desk without rising, introduced himself, and gestured for Landry to sit.

With a smile he asked the purpose of Landry's visit.

"I hoped you might be hiring. I have a journalism degree, and I'd like to find work in my field." He handed his brief résumé over, and the editor glanced at it.

"Deputy sheriff, eh? You had to have pretty good benefits and a decent salary too. But you quit. Was that your idea or your boss's?"

Here we go. Landry explained that he was researching old cases while having nothing else to do on the night shift, and he was told to stop. Thinking he was onto something that might break a series of cold cases, he kept looking, got caught and was terminated. It was basically the truth, although if contacted, the sheriff might reveal a few more facts, like breaking and entering and disobeying a direct order, and that would be a big problem.

"Doing a little investigating in your spare time, eh? I can only imagine how quiet the night shift would be in the sheriff's office of a small parish like ours. If I call the sheriff and ask for a reference, what do you think he'll say?"

He couldn't lose what he didn't have anyway. "He'll say he told me to quit looking at the database, he took away my notes that I spent hours creating, and I went into his office on a different night and tried to find them. When I couldn't, I spent the rest of my shift trying to recreate the notes by searching the same database he ordered me to stay out of."

The editor looked at Landry for a long time, the hint of a smile on his face. "Will he say anything else? Are you going to be charged with a crime? Is there anything else I should know?"

"I don't know for sure," Landry admitted. "I can't imagine what I did is serious enough for that. I think he was mad that I disobeyed him. I shouldn't have done it, but I was onto something, Mr. Jones. I'm not one to create trouble, and I know how to obey orders. If you'll give me a chance, I'll do any job you have just so I can work. I need the money, to tell the truth."

The editor said, "Let me tell you a few things, and then I have a question for you. First, the pay in the journalism business is notoriously low unless you're Woodward or Bernstein, know what I mean? Nobody, including the editor — that's me — makes much money. Second, I don't have any permanent openings. I do have a copy editor who's going on maternity leave. She'll be out six or eight weeks, but I definitely want her back. I want a temp for her position, since it will only last a few weeks. Third, I'm intrigued by what you thought you found in that database, and that brings me to my question. What were you looking for, and what did you find?"

His question took Landry by surprise. He'd felt a glimmer of hope when Mr. Jones mentioned the copy editor position, because it sounded as if he might hire Landry on a temporary basis without checking with the sheriff. But now he was in a quandary. Why did this man want to know about the things he'd learned? He paused to collect his thoughts.

"I saw a number of seemingly unrelated cases that happened in one particular place over many years. They were violent crimes, and I found something that was a common thread — something that tied them all together. Some cases went cold years ago, but I think they're related. I can understand the sheriff doesn't have the resources to open up a big can of worms, and he probably didn't want the state police nosing around his office looking into something a rookie deputy turned up. I get it, but I'm onto something."

The editor's face looked eager. The journalist in him wanted more. "Where did these violent crimes happen?"

Landry had anticipated this question as he was talking. "If I worked for this newspaper, I'd tell you everything and hope you'd let me keep working on the cases. Until then, I can't tell you anything more. I'm still working on some angles, and I want to keep things to myself for now."

"Damn," the editor replied with a laugh. "You really know how to do a job interview! If the *Daily Iberian* were large enough for an investigative reporter, I'd hire you on the spot!"

The editor explained what he was willing to do. He would contact the sheriff and get his version of the termination. If Landry's story was substantially factual, he could have the temporary copy editor's job at twelve dollars an hour. In exchange, Landry would tell Jones everything.

He could keep investigating, and the paper would pay him up to ten hours a week of overtime in exchange for an exclusive story if things worked out. The story would be his to ferret out; a seasoned reporter would help him write it, but it would carry Landry's byline.

Everything sounded great to Landry, and he was told to expect a call once the editor contacted Sheriff Barbour. He cautioned that even though he would get on it right away, it might take a while to get in touch with the sheriff.

Even though the pay was far lower, Landry was excited about what the editor had offered. If his hunches were right, his name would be on a page one story. Best of all, with a job he could pay his rent on time.

All that had to happen was one satisfactory response from a man who had summarily dismissed him and threatened to charge him with breaking and entering, a felony that might have gotten him sent to prison.

FORGOTTEN MEN: THE BAYOU HAUNTINGS

He put all that aside for now, took out his blue blazer and tan slacks, and mentally prepared himself for an interesting evening with Cate's dad.

CHAPTER SEVENTEEN

Landry drove through the entry gate to Rip Van Winkle Gardens at a quarter to seven. He passed a black BMW 7-series sedan with Texas plates parked next to a quaint cottage, walked in the restaurant, and identified himself to a hostess. She took him to their patio table, where they were having drinks.

Cate waved and her father stood as Landry approached the table. Madison John Adams was a tall man with a rugged, tanned face that showed he spent lots of time outdoors. He put out his hand, introduced himself, told Landry everyone called him Doc, and offered the chair between him and his daughter. As Landry sat, she squeezed his hand.

A waiter took Landry's order for a rum and Coke, and Doc said, "Cate tells me you're on the sheriff's force in this parish. How do you like it?"

Landry didn't want to discuss his termination tonight, not during his first meeting with Cate's father. "It's interesting, but I'm looking for a better fit. I have a journalism degree, but I don't know if I can use it around here. I'm not worried; something will come along."

The answer satisfied them, and Doc changed the subject.

"We'll chat about the island later, but first I'd like to know your thoughts about the Asylum."

There could be no secrets from Doc because he owned the property and Landry needed permission to go there. Now and then as he talked, Cate's dad nodded and smiled. Intrigued by the story, he wanted more.

They paused the conversation for dinner, and Landry commented that this was the best fish he'd ever eaten. Also probably the most expensive, but he kept that comment to himself.

They finished, and the questions began. Doc wondered what was significant about June 10. Murders happened some years, but not others. Were they connected? He was analytical, accustomed to probing a situation to learn the answers. Landry answered tough questions the best he could. The time flew by; Landry was having a great time with someone who shared his enthusiasm for mysteries.

Doc asked for any other thoughts, no matter how far-fetched and crazy.

"He could be a serial killer," Landry replied, and the three of them discussed that idea. A serial killer staying busy for thirty years? Unlikely, but what if it were true? Who could it be? Someone who lived in the area, a man — or less likely a woman — who had neighbors and a family, who could hide an appetite for gruesome murders for decades? Serial killers typically worked alone, but could there have been two of them?

Clearly accustomed to fine dining, Doc knew how to make things happen. He requested little extras here and there — some special sauce Landry didn't know and an order of haricots verts. Landry kept his mouth closed; when the dish arrived, he learned that haricots verts were green beans with French butter.

Once servers cleared the plates, Doc asked if Landry would join him in a brandy and a coffee. "Cate won't do it, I can already tell you." He laughed. "She and her mother prefer something with a little less bite to it."

Landry would have too, but he'd never tried brandy, so he joined his host. When the snifters came, he followed Doc's lead, swirling it around for a moment before taking a whiff. To him it smelled like rubbing alcohol. He should have watched Doc take a little sip and savor it, but instead Landry took a swig, wincing when the stuff burned like fire all the way down his throat.

Next came a brief coughing spell. As he composed himself, they chuckled, then apologized for laughing, and he said in future he'd skip after-dinner drinks. Cate suggested he give her Baileys a try. He took a sip and found it refreshing, cool and delicious. It was everything the brandy wasn't. Doc signaled the waiter, ordered him one, and poured the rest of Landry's brandy into his own snifter, saying it'd be a shame for it to go to waste.

They talked about the island. Cate's father said he wanted to look the place over and use a metal detector he'd brought. "I'm a total amateur at detecting," he said, "but I've found small things with this machine in the past. My thought is that we go out there tomorrow, spend a few hours getting our bearings, and come up with a plan. I've got a contact in Houston who's a professional metal detector — he works for one of the major oil companies, and he's got sophisticated equipment that's turned up some very interesting finds. If things look promising, I'll call in the big guns."

They agreed to meet tomorrow morning at a boat landing in Charenton, just a few miles away from the little island called Lafitte Landing. Doc had rented a motorboat, and Landry said he'd bring a cooler with water, sodas and beer. Around ten, Doc settled the tab. As she and her dad left the restaurant, Cate surprised him with a peck on the cheek.

That night Landry tossed and turned, his dreams so vivid they occasionally woke him. In one scenario, the sheriff and a crew of gun-toting deputies marched into the *Daily Iberian* and arrested him at his desk, taking him away in handcuffs as coworkers watched in horror.

In another, Cate, her father and Landry found a wooden box full of gold beneath a tree marked with an X and a skull and crossbones. That one would have been laughable if there hadn't been a terrifying encounter with a specter as they realized they were digging on the night of June tenth.

Landry rose before daybreak, checked his email, and saw nothing from the *Daily Iberian*. He put a cooler in the Jeep, stopped by the QuikTrip to buy drinks and ice, and was on his way to Charenton.

Doc ran the outboard motor and steered the craft down the Teche. Landry sat in the front of the boat, and Cate was in the middle. Every time he turned around, she gave him a big smile. It was a gorgeous morning, perfect for bird watching, fishing, boating or even treasure hunting. He thought life would be perfect if he got a text message right about now offering him that job.

They pulled up on a rocky beach, tied the boat, and found one trail that led into the underbrush. Doc had a satellite map of the area, so even though the island had lots of trees, they knew where the cabin was, and soon they emerged into a clearing where Hank's man cave stood. The front door was open, and someone was whistling inside.

Doc led the way, stepping onto the porch and knocking on the door.

"Go away! No trespassing!"

"I couldn't agree more," Doc replied. "Come outside so we can see you."

In a moment a tall, thin man with a pencil mustache stepped onto the porch. He wore a flannel shirt, jeans and work boots, and he was holding a shotgun.

His voice was deep and powerful. "What are you doing here? Can't you read the signs down by the water? No trespassing! Now get out!"

"How about I ask the questions?" Cate's father shot back. "What are you doing here?"

The man paused for a moment. "This is my place."

"And just who are you?"

"Ezekiel Billings. Reverend Ezekiel Billings to you."

"What makes you think you own this island, Reverend Billings?" Landry was impressed; Doc hadn't backed off one bit.

"Tell me again who you are?"

"I'm Madison Adams. Dr. Madison Adams to you. I own the property. You're the trespasser, so how about you tell me what you're doing here."

Billings stood his ground for a moment, and they were unsure what was coming next. Doc was less than five feet from him, while Landry and Cate were farther away, off the porch. Landry was wondering what he'd do if the guy raised the shotgun, but at last Billings walked over to a wooden table and put it down.

His tone of voice became more cordial. "I thought it didn't belong to anybody. It used to belong to some football player, but he died years ago."

"So you decided to make it yours?"

"There was no one to ask, and no one to stop me, Dr. Adams. I've been coming out here for two years, maybe longer. It's my little getaway."

Doc said, "How about we go into my cabin and talk, Reverend Billings."

The place was neat, clean and habitable. He directed them to a table in the main room. Billings explained that he was an evangelist who preached in small churches all over southern Louisiana. He said he lived in New Orleans and came here to unwind between the revivals he conducted. He heard there was a cabin, and he had found it, complete with furniture and everything else he needed.

"I paid to turn the utilities back on, and I've spent a few days every month here ever since. The guy who built it — the football player — died, and I guess everything is just like it was when he left it for the last time. What brought you all out here?"

"I bought it three years ago. I live over in Galveston, and I've never been here. We decided to check it out today. I asked my daughter and her friend to join me."

"That's a fancy metal detector you have," Billings replied, recalling the boys and their father earlier, who had one too. "Looking for something in particular?"

"That's none of your business. You have to go. I have plans for the place, and they don't include you. Take whatever's yours and get off my island. Where's your boat?"

"In a cove on the back side."

"I'll give you twenty-four hours to gather your stuff and get out. Leave everything that you found here; those things belong to me."

Billings's face turned red. "Not a neighborly sort, are ya?"

Doc smiled. "I don't greet guests on the porch with a shotgun, if that's what you mean. I've changed my mind about the twenty-four-hour deadline. Be off this island by five. If I catch you here again, I'll call the sheriff."

The preacher fumed as he gathered his things, putting them on the table.

As Landry, Cate and Doc Adams walked to the door, Billings muttered, "We'll run into each other again. Maybe I can teach you a little something about being neighborly when that happens."

"That might not be such a good idea, Reverend. A restraining order wouldn't enhance your preaching career."

They walked out, leaving the man to his packing.

"Wow, Dad!" Cate exclaimed. "Well done! Think we've seen the last of him?"

"Without a doubt. People like that are all full of bluster, but they're harmless when it comes down to putting up or shutting up. He won't be back."

While they waited for him to vacate the cabin, they explored the island. It was so covered with vegetation there wasn't a good spot to try the detector. They walked the shoreline instead, and Doc ran it back and forth, hoping to unearth things people had dropped.

He had warned them that the machine would locate all metal, including plenty of modern stuff. "Don't get your hopes up just because we get a lot of hits," he said. As he predicted, the machine buzzed almost every time he directed it over the surface. They found bottle caps, tinfoil, pop-tops and coins. Their biggest discovery was a silver ring that once held a stone. It wasn't worth much, but it was the only thing they located that wasn't debris.

They stopped for lunch, sitting under a tree and eating the ham and cheese sandwiches Cate had ordered from the restaurant that morning. Landry took drink orders and passed out the beer and sodas from the cooler. A nice breeze came through the trees, and she said it was fun to be treasure hunting on a little island.

Her dad smiled. "Always the optimist. We find enough junk to fill a trash bag, and in your eyes, we're having a great time looking for gold!"

"I have to agree with her," Landry commented. "I've spent worse Saturdays than this."

They leaned back against trees and relaxed. Doc pulled a cigar from his shirt pocket, clipped and lit it and took a long, satisfying puff. "Care to join me?" he asked. "I brought two."

"No, sir. After the brandy episode last night, I'd better pass. I tried cigarettes in high school like everyone else, but my smoking was actually just coughing. It didn't work for me."

"As a medical doctor, I always urge people not to smoke. However —" he took another drag "— a nice Cuban cigar that draws like this one can help a man calm down and quit thinking about his problems. It's a cathartic release for me."

"Oh, Dad." Cate laughed. "That's such a bunch of bull. You've been smoking cigars since before I was born. What big problems do you have that require a cigar for a cathartic release? Tell the truth. You're a cigar snob. You like Cubans because they're hard to get and you can impress your friends when you give them one. Right?"

"You're being way too hard on me! I'm not a snob. I enjoy the finer things in life. Frankly, this Cuban would be much more enjoyable right now if you'd quit harping at me about it." He smiled and winked at Landry.

"Not to interrupt this family banter," Landry interjected. "but what's the plan now? Are we going to keep looking?"

Doc wanted to stay until Reverend Billings left the island. Once they heard his boat, they'd go back to Charenton, and he and Cate would return home. They'd be in Galveston by dark.

Humiliated and angry, Ezekiel Billings made several trips through the woods, carrying his things to his boat. Humility wasn't part of his makeup. Anger was, and he would deal with that condescending doctor who kicked him off the island that had been his home for many months. He always found vengeance to be a satisfying thing, and he smiled as he recalled the "eye for an eye, tooth for a tooth" story from the Bible. Instead of turning the other cheek, he repaid his enemies. Dr. Adams was an enemy now. His daughter and her friend too. They were all in this together.

Around three, Doc, Landry and Cate heard a motorboat — noisy at first, then soft as it went away. Having found nothing significant using the detector, they walked to the cabin, gave it a walk-through, shut the front door and left. Doc asked his daughter to help him remember to bring a padlock next time.

Landry said goodbye in the parking lot at Charenton. He was sincere when he told Doc how much he'd enjoyed getting to know him, and what a great time he had last night and today. Not sure what to expect from Cate, he stuck out his hand, but she gave him a tight hug and said she'd call Monday.

"I'm off; call anytime," he replied, and it was the truth. There was no job anymore. He regretted not telling her, but he hadn't wanted to bring it up in front of her father. He would explain everything soon.

His apartment was claustrophobic and lonely after a day outside with her. Now he faced another Saturday night alone, as usual. In bed, he thought how important the editor's call was in his life. It was critical, but the call that he looked forward to was the one she promised him on Monday.

He hadn't felt like this about a girl in a long time.

Ever, to be honest.

He fell asleep with a smile on his face and dreamed about a beautiful girl, a little kiss, and the embrace as they parted.

CHAPTER EIGHTEEN

The next morning Landry performed his Sunday ritual. He took his laptop to Starbucks, ordered a coffee and muffin, and caught up on the news. At the Winn-Dixie an hour later, he bought chips, soft drinks, water and beer. Buying a few groceries at this point didn't bother him. If the job at the *Iberian* didn't work out, he'd be doing something else soon. He'd decide by end of day tomorrow. If the job didn't pan out, he'd hit the streets Tuesday morning. Fry cook, ditchdigger, truck unloader — he didn't know what it would be, but he'd be working this week.

That afternoon he spent five bucks going to a movie he didn't really care about. He was just killing time. When he left the theater, he turned his phone off mute and heard several dings. He looked at his incoming mail and his adrenalin flowed. Excited, he read Ty Jones's mail. It turned out to be nothing to get that excited about, but it gave him hope anyway.

"Hey, Landry. I spoke with Sheriff Barbour. If you have time, please come by this afternoon. I'll be here until four.

Otherwise we can get together tomorrow afternoon around two if that works for you."

He looked at his watch: it was a quarter to five, but he called anyway in hopes Jones might still be there. A recorded greeting said the office was closed.

Crap! I should have kept my phone on!

He wondered if he should call the editor at home, but he decided against it. Although he wanted the job, he didn't want to seem desperate. Who knew what the sheriff had said? There might not even be a job offer. Either way, as frustrating as it would be, he had to wait.

His night consisted of little sleep and hours awake. He tried to stay busy in the morning, but at last it was time. He walked in at two, and the editor waved him back.

Jones asked if Landry wanted the job, and he said he did.

"I want to give you a couple of days doing copyediting so we can see how suited you are for the position. If it all works out, the job is yours. I have one request. I know it's asking a lot, but if you accept the post, will you promise me you won't bail on me until my copy editor returns to work? You might make more money somewhere else, and you might miss an opportunity, but I need this position filled, period. In return, I'll promise that if you do well and something full time opens that fits your skill set, you'll be the first one I talk to."

"That sounds great, and I appreciate the chance. When do I start?"

"Come with me. I'll introduce you to Helene. She's the one you'll be filling in for, and I'd like for you to start tomorrow morning so you can have time with her before her baby arrives."

Landry agreed, and as they stood, he said, "I'm curious about something. You may not want to answer, but can you tell me what the sheriff said?"

"He said by law he couldn't discuss personnel matters. He verified that you had been a deputy but not another word, positive or negative. I assumed you told me the truth, so here you are. Welcome aboard!"

When Cate called later that afternoon, he explained everything. He apologized for stretching the truth at dinner. No worries, she said, congratulating him and saying the job might just work into something he'd enjoy long-term.

She said she and her father had enjoyed the evening and asked if he'd come to Galveston soon to spend a day or two. That sounded good, and they agreed to talk more once he settled in to his new job.

Landry and the pregnant copy editor squeezed into her cramped cubicle. He took furious notes as she went from subject to subject, explaining her duties. She appeared to be genuinely interested in helping him. After three days working with Landry, she told the editor his progress and intelligence impressed her.

On Friday two exciting things happened. First thing that morning, a man stopped by their cubicle and handed out white envelopes.

"Payday," Helene exclaimed. "Most fun day of the week!"

You have no idea, Landry thought to himself. The check had come just in time.

Four hours later, Helene rushed to the restroom and returned to announce her baby was on its way. Sooner than expected, Landry became the new temporary copy editor.

The newspaper didn't print a Sunday edition, so the office closed from noon Saturday until first thing Monday morning. Landry worked weekdays from seven until two, but most days the paper went to press early and his editing work was over. He had free time every day after noon, and he spent it researching the Asylum's history.

One afternoon Landry's boss stopped by his desk. He praised Landry on how he got his work done efficiently. Since he had dead time some days, Ty had something for him to work on. Next year was Iberia Parish's sesquicentennial, with a yearlong celebration of its hundred and fiftieth birthday. The *Daily Iberian*'s contribution to the festivities would be a series of articles about the parish, its history, towns and citizens.

"Most of my staff already have topics," he explained. "They'll research, gather historical information, find pictures and other relevant stuff, and write a six-thousand-word article about their subject. We'll run two articles a month. At the end, we'll compile them into a coffee-table book people can buy."

The project sounded interesting, and he hoped it might mean job security. If his boss wanted him to research and write an article, maybe this was a trial run for a permanent position. He said he appreciated the opportunity and offered to write about the mysterious deaths he'd researched.

Landry's boss smiled and shook his head. "That would be a perfect topic for you, but I spent two tough months refining this project until the editorial board and my publisher approved it. There's a lot of people's time and energy involved in this. They chose the topics some time ago. Here's the one I'd like you to tackle. What do you think?"

He handed Landry a sheet of paper with five words on it, and Landry broke into a grin. He would have preferred the Asylum, but if he couldn't do that, this one worked just fine.

"It's a great topic," he said with a grin. "I'll get started right now."

His topic — the Treasure of Bayou Teche — was perfect. He turned to his computer, learned that Frank Connolly had owned not only the Hotel Iberia but an island nearby, and began to take notes.

CHAPTER NINETEEN

Summer 1820
Victory, Louisiana

No one in Victory knew where Frank Connolly originated. His personality didn't lend itself to idle talk about himself — or anyone else. His life before he arrived in town was a mystery. In reality, he was born in 1758 back East somewhere, moved to New Orleans around 1800, and started a trading company in the busy port city. He did well, and by 1810 he was making a modest living.

Like Frank, many other traders worked out of warehouses along the docks. One was a man of dubious character named Jean Lafitte. Like everyone else in New Orleans, Frank heard stories about Jean and his brother Pierre; he'd even met them once at some merchants' meeting. Some said the Lafitte brothers were pirates and claimed Jean's warehouses along the Mississippi River were brimful of stolen goods.

A year later, Jean closed his New Orleans operation and moved everything to new warehouses on an island down near the Gulf of Mexico. Some said he moved because the police were about to arrest him. Others thought the brothers moved from the city to a less-populated area to continue their trade without interference.

The Lafitte legend extended far beyond New Orleans. Southwestern Louisiana teemed with lakes and rivers, and trappers often showed up at Frank's door with furs to sell. He bought their goods, bought them drinks, and listened to wild stories about the Lafitte brothers. The grizzly outdoorsmen claimed to have seen Jean Lafitte moving cargo in a barge up a river called the Teche. One man told Frank the cargo was precious gems, gold and silver, things too valuable to keep in a warehouse. The pirate was hiding the good stuff, he said.

Frank didn't believe him. No pirate would let others see his loot. But he listened because the tales were interesting.

A man commented that as he ran traps along the Teche, he'd seen a longboat so heavy with cargo it was almost underwater. Lafitte and his men were heading north; the pirate had even tipped his hat as they passed by. Two days later, the boat returned, southbound and empty.

The tales continued, because the trappers didn't spend much time around others. When they made a rare trip to town, their stories made the locals take notice, and they liked the attention.

Frank didn't talk a lot himself, but he enjoyed a good story. Enough of these tales had common threads that he decided to see the river for himself.

He paid a trapper twenty dollars to take him up the Teche to where Lafitte's barge had supposedly passed by. On the way, the man showed Frank a few of the bayou's islands, and a few days later they returned to New Orleans. After that, Frank made the trip several more times alone.

Frank must have found something because by 1812, just two years later, he left New Orleans to move to a small town called Victory, which lay along the Teche River. He paid in gold coins for a thirty-acre plot of riverfront property and a small island next to it. He also filed a charter to start a bank with a hundred thousand dollars of capital — every dollar of which he provided himself.

Somehow, a simple trader had become the wealthiest man in southwestern Louisiana in just two years. No one connected his sudden prosperity to his trips west. No one knew Frank well in New Orleans, so no one raised an eyebrow. He closed his trading company, left the big city, and appeared one day as a rich man in a small town. He hired a crew to clear brush on his property, he posted no-trespassing signs on his island, and he began construction on the tallest building in downtown Victory. It opened in 1815 with the words *Connolly Investments* etched in stone across the top — a monument to himself.

Connolly came to Victory alone. He had no wife or family, and his reclusive nature kept him from cultivating close friendships. The townspeople understood, because his money set him apart from everyone else. When he passed them on the street, they gave a little bow and said hello. The lucky ones got a hello back. Most of the time Frank walked on, deep in thought, working through one of his big business deals, people assumed.

The fewer things folks know about a prominent person, the more stories they make up. Locals wondered about the millionaire's past and made conclusions based on few solid facts. Frank had said he'd been a merchant and trader in New Orleans before coming to Victory. From that single tidbit arose a theory. Wasn't Jean Lafitte a trader in New Orleans too? Had he met him? Were they in cahoots?

He built the only brick buildings in town — one for his bank, and his headquarters, a three-story office building. He maintained an apartment on the top floor. His housekeeper spoke of beautiful sculptures on pedestals and paintings on the walls, but only she ever entered Frank's private domain.

In 1816 the town's councilmen asked Connolly to run for mayor. Given his financial commitment to the area, he was the logical choice, and he accepted with a caveat. He refused to stand for election. If he had no opponents, they could appoint him instead of his running for office. Two men's names were already on the ballot, and civic leaders took them aside for a little talk. They withdrew from the race, and Frank Connolly became the mayor of Victory, a position he would hold for many years. After 1820, when he opened his hotel, the town became so dependent upon him for its economic livelihood that he was a virtual dictator. Nothing happened unless Frank wanted it, and most things Frank approved of made his wallet even fatter.

By the early summer of 1824, his hotel had become a success beyond Frank's wildest dreams. The town thrived too, and as the czar of the community, Frank made sure no competitors impeded his personal goals. Two other groups filed charters for banks in Victory, a sign of the area's prosperity, but over dinner at the hotel, Frank convinced the state banking commissioner to deny the applications. As long as Victory existed, his would be the only bank in town.

"Massa Connolly! Massa Connolly! Come quick!"

Frank's eyes blazed with anger as one of his men ran across the lawn. He yelled at the top of his lungs, piercing the reverie and irritating Frank no end. He was having a sweet tea with lemon on the veranda with a senator and his wife from Shreveport, who were enjoying a complimentary weekend in the presidential suite here at the Hotel Iberia.

Connolly disliked interruptions. He disliked so many things that some people called him antisocial. Regardless, the townspeople who received benefit themselves from the money the hotel brought to the area held Frank in high regard. Likewise, his guests endured their host's eccentricities. His brusque demeanor and habit of interrupting everyone should have irritated them, but they said nothing. He owned the ritziest establishment in the South, and his invitations were impossible to decline. If there was to be a grand ball at Frank's hotel, everyone wanted an invitation despite the owner's unorthodox social skills.

"What is it, man? Can't you see I'm with friends?"

The man stopped ten feet from the veranda. The outside help wasn't allowed any closer, and his clothes were damp from sweat. He wiped his brow with his sleeve and said, "This can't wait, sir! The men — they's found somethin' new!"

"It must be something special to get him into such a tizzy." Connolly laughed as he excused himself and walked down the steps and over to his man. They spoke in whispers for a moment, and he returned to his guests. Offering his regrets, he explained that there was a pressing issue he needed to attend to. He left the couple and walked with his employee to the river, where they got into a rowboat.

The servant, a freedman and trusted employee named Moses, rowed across the Bayou Teche toward the nearby island Frank owned. Over several days, two men had been clearing brush and looking for something. Frank didn't have to ask if they'd found it. He could see it in Moses's face.

The man led his boss through the trees until they reached a clearing. Two of Frank's most trusted men sat under a tree, naked from the waist up and glistening with sweat. When the big boss arrived, they stood and removed their hats. Their show of respect wasn't voluntary; Frank demanded his workers perform that ritual when he came into their presence.

"Did they find a rock?" he asked, and Moses pointed to a large flat stone lying nearby.

Frank knelt and ran his finger along several deep marks on the rock's surface — a combination of letters and numbers. Even if his men could read and write, they wouldn't have understood what the symbols meant. Only Frank could interpret them because he'd seen a similar inscription twelve years ago on a different part of this island. When the old trapper showed Frank the rock in 1812, Frank had copied the symbols and gone back to New Orleans to study them.

It had taken weeks of frustrating mental energy to decipher the letters and numbers. They were a map — a key to finding something buried on the island. Before long he made his first solo trip back to Bayou Teche, followed the map, and dug a four-foot-deep hole.

What Frank Connolly unearthed transformed him from a middle-class merchant to a wealthy man. He removed a strongbox from the hole and replaced the dirt so it looked undisturbed. The box had been there for years. Perhaps Lafitte wasn't coming back for it. Rumor was that the brothers had left Louisiana to become spies for the Spanish in Mexico's fight for independence. They could be dead by now.

Frank never spoke of the box. He sold jewels now and then when he needed money, but he stashed away most of the gold since it was legal tender. To avoid creating attention, he never visited the same merchant twice to sell his things. He transferred hard assets into currency repeatedly until his bank account — and several safety-deposit boxes — brimmed with cash and gold coins.

Today, Frank's men had found another rock, another inscription and another key to a hidden cache. Now he knew the Lafitte brothers had been here at least twice. This truly was their treasure island. After he decrypted the code Lafitte had scratched into the stone, Connolly's men dug up another box. To buy their silence, Frank gave each of them a hundred-dollar gold coin. It was a fortune to the workers, but it was a pittance compared to what lay inside the box.

After that, Frank occasionally sent a crew to search for more engraved rocks, but none turned up. Since no one knew Frank had found two caches, the legend remained alive.

Connolly left Louisiana in 1838. He took his possessions some place up North by train. People in New Iberia watched as men coupled Frank's fancy private rail car to an engine. Armed security guards were everywhere, keeping sightseers back and ensuring Mr. Connolly's privacy and safety. When the train pulled out of the station, the guards went along. They would stay with their boss until he reached his new home.

People commented how much security Mr. Connolly had that day. They thought he was the wealthiest man in this parish, but no one imagined the truth. He was by far the richest man in the South, thanks to Jean Lafitte.

Two hundred years later, amateur treasure hunters still explored Lafitte Landing in hopes they'd find pirate booty. No one knew Frank had already dug up two caches. Could Lafitte have made more trips to the island? The Treasure of

Bayou Teche might still be there, waiting for a metal detector to signal that the person holding it was a millionaire.

CHAPTER TWENTY

"If you're good to God, God's gonna be good to you! If you believe, shout AMEN!"

"AMEN!" came the thunderous response that shook the little church building.

"What you give to help others comes back to help you tenfold. If you believe Jesus Christ wants to help you, shout AMEN!"

Again there was a roar interspersed with hallelujahs, and fifty pairs of hands waved in the air.

"Amen! Amen, my brothers and sisters!" The preacher slammed his Bible onto the pulpit so hard that a cup of water sitting on it fell off and splashed upon the stage. His hair was soaked with sweat; Ezekiel gave his all to his little congregations. His presence mesmerized his listeners — his voice was so powerful and so charismatic that the words he bellowed paralyzed the folks sitting in the pews. Some of them swore it was like hearing the voice of God Himself.

Ezekiel Billings swaggered across the stage and sat down. The regular pastor walked to the podium and instructed the deacons to collect tonight's offering — a love offering for Brother Billings so he could keep the message of Jesus Christ alive among the people of southern Louisiana.

As ushers passed the collection plates, the choir sang a rousing version of "When We All Get to Heaven," their joyful faces and dancing feet showing how happy they were to be here in the Ebenezer Baptist Church of Lydia, Louisiana. The little sanctuary had been packed for each of the three nights for his spiritual revival filled with fire and brimstone. On those warm summer evenings, latecomers stood outside at the open windows on the sides, getting into the fervor of the sermon just like those who were fortunate enough to have come an hour early for a seat in the pews.

Billings wasn't a Baptist preacher. He wasn't even an ordained minister. He was a charismatic, confident and captivating individual whose striking good looks and powerful voice drew people to him. An hour of his Bible-thumping, hellfire doomsday preaching could make even the most dedicated Christian come down front at invitation time, rededicating his life to the Savior just in case it hadn't taken the last time. Reverend Billings was a master at getting them to open their pocketbooks too. There was nothing like the fear of eternal damnation to make a man try to buy his way to glory.

Ezekiel Billings didn't have a church of his own. He was a traveling evangelist, one of many who visited small fundamentalist congregations in rural communities. Nobody knew how Billings had started. He showed up one day a few years back, making the rounds through tiny communities, offering to come in and put on a soul-stirring revival for whatever "love offering" the congregation put into the collection plate on his last night in town.

Small-town pastors were only too happy to have someone dynamic take the stage for a few evenings, save a few souls to add to the flock of God's chosen people, generate a little extra cash for both the church and himself, and move on down the road.

When he arrived, one of the church members housed the itinerant preacher for the few nights he was in town. The minute word got out Reverend Billings was coming, the sign-up sheet at church for members who'd host a lunch or dinner filled up in minutes. People were eager to get to know the flamboyant, boisterous minister better than their fellow parishioners who missed an opportunity to be up close and personal with one of God's spokesmen.

The revival in Lydia turned out to be one of Ezekiel Billings's most profitable ones. After the first night of his revival, Brother and Sister Trahan were his hosts for dinner. The service had been powerful and moving, and it thrilled them to have him to themselves. As in every other town, Billings had done his homework on the people who lived there, and he knew something about Marcus Trahan that might be helpful to him ... and to God's continuing work on Earth.

"I don't care a whit about worldly possessions myself," he said between mouthfuls of Sister Trahan's excellent pot roast, her signature mashed potatoes and some scrumptious brown gravy. His sincerity and humility warmed the hearts of the captivated couple, who — fortuitously for Reverend Billings — owned the only car dealership around. He laughed. "Old Betsy's goin' to Heaven, I fear. She's got a hundred and ninety thousand miles on her, and I'm afraid she'll die on me before I can get to Maurice for my next revival. The work of the Lord requires putting a lot of miles on my car, and good old Betsy won't make it much longer."

"Let me work on that for you," Brother Trahan had said, patting the evangelist's arm and glad he could be of help to this fine preacher. "God just gave me a sign."

Whether that sign had come from Heaven or from Reverend Billings, the pastor who'd arrived in Lydia driving an old clunker left town the proud owner of a much nicer one — a 2010 Ford F-150 pickup with less than forty thousand miles on it.

That went well, he thought to himself as he said goodbye to new friends in Lydia and turned onto the highway for the thirty-minute drive to Maurice. Nine hundred and ninety dollars in the offering plate and a pickup worth maybe fifteen thousand dollars. One of his oft-repeated points during sermons was that God helps those who help themselves, and this time — like many times before — a faithful church member wanting to solidify his place in Heaven gave a poor preacher man something he needed. Billings smiled, reached into his jacket pocket, pulled out a flask, and took a hefty swig.

A thousand bucks for three days of doing something so easy I don't even have to think about it. I even use the same throwaway phrases — the same fear-of-damnation words — in every little church. Who'd have thought this was possible? He drank from the flask again and reached into his briefcase for a bottle of mouthwash. Half an hour from now he'd be at his next stop, and when he met the good people at Chimney Hill Pentecostal Church, his breath had to smell ... well, heavenly.

CHAPTER TWENTY-ONE

Reverend Billings didn't believe in the supernatural. To tell the truth, he didn't believe in much of anything except how much more intelligent and crafty he was than every other human. For all that Bible-thumping talk about Jesus and Satan and eternal life in glory and burning in Hell for your sins, Reverend Billings didn't believe a word. It was all part of the spiel — the sales pitch — that got him the cash he needed to keep his modest lifestyle. He didn't need much money, but there had been times when he had none. What he did now — earning a living telling a bunch of evangelicals what they wanted to hear — sure beat rummaging through trash bins behind restaurants or siphoning gas in the dead of night.

Billings had always been a cynic. He trusted no one, he liked no one, and he damned sure didn't depend on anyone but himself. At dinners with members of the little churches after a service, they'd comment on his passion and love of the Word. Then they'd ask why he preached out here in the boonies instead of in the metropolitan churches like those in Baton Rouge or New Orleans.

"You're so charismatic, Reverend," a lady said as she passed the biscuits and gravy one evening. "You have such a powerful message. Although I thank God you've chosen to share it with us here in Berwick, why, you'd reach more sinners in a week in a city than we have people in our whole town!"

He smiled, thanked her for the kind words in his syrupy, sincere-sounding voice, and reminded her we were all called by God to do his bidding. "He's not asking me to be a Billy Graham. He's called me to minister in towns like yours, to reach people who won't drive to New Orleans to listen to a preacher. I don't need worldly possessions. I'm content to do what I do. If it suits God, it suits me!"

The parishioners had no idea there wasn't a single word of truth to anything he said. Ezekiel Billings stayed out of the limelight for one reason only — people in the city sometimes asked difficult questions, ones that might change his career yet again. Things like a biography, or references, or a list of the schools and seminaries he had attended — those difficult things kept Ezekiel out of the big churches.

It was a shame how bad things had gotten these days, he sometimes mused. Nobody trusted anybody, especially big-city people, who saw terrorists and child molesters in every stranger. It wasn't that way in rural Louisiana, thank God. When a town of four thousand souls was graced by the presence of a mighty servant of the Lord, nobody asked for references. The success of his fire-and-brimstone revivals over the past year or so served as reference enough. The word spread; in tiny towns, people were thrilled he'd deigned to visit their churches, giving them a rousing, soul-saving revival in exchange for nothing really — food, lodging and a love offering.

Speaking of love offerings, sometimes Reverend Billings had to rein in the love. When he stayed at Brother and Sister so-and-so's house, and their teenaged daughter had to give up her room for a couple of days, he behaved himself, although sometimes he looked through her personal things just for the thrill of seeing what the girl wore under her modest dress.

Other times women made offers he would have loved to accept. As hard as it was, Ezekiel had to resist. For instance, there had been that one night in a two-bit town when there was a soft knock at two a.m. Wearing a lacy nightie, the wife opened the door, stuck her head inside, and asked if he needed anything.

Yes, he did, but Ezekiel resisted as always. As much as he wanted to accept the tacit invitation and invite her in, he thanked her and shook his head.

"Just finishing my prayers, my dear sister. All good here. See you in the morning."

He hated to let willing women walk away, but he couldn't risk even one impropriety. His story was constructed on such shallow footings that it wouldn't stand up to even the most basic inquiry. One accusation by an angry husband, followed by the local pastor looking into Ezekiel's past — that would be a situation that could end the gravy train. When he was Billings the traveling evangelist, he must keep immodest impulses in check. When he was out of character, he did whatever he wanted.

CHAPTER TWENTY-TWO

Ezekiel Billings came back to the Asylum because he'd come another time, when he needed a place to lie low until things blew over. He hadn't seen the massive old building in a while, and he walked around outside in the dark, thinking the place didn't seem as forbidding and frightening as the last time. Someone was inside — homeless people or kids. He heard quiet voices, laughter and smelled weed as he passed empty windows. Since they were here, he couldn't go inside tonight. He couldn't risk running into someone who might recognize him.

When he returned a few days later, the trespassers had left. Everything was as quiet as a drafty, creaking, moaning, two-hundred-year-old structure could be. He walked through the former prison, remembering the last time he came.

Ezekiel's friend said he sometimes stayed in a basement here, but you never knew when to believe him. He said a lot of strange things, and Ezekiel figured about ninety percent wasn't true.

His friend said you got to the basement through a closet in a detached kitchen that led to a stairway, and Ezekiel wanted to see for himself. He walked out the back and down the stairs, crossed the yard, and entered the only other building left standing — a one-story wooden structure in better shape than the main one.

He searched everywhere and found nothing that led to a basement. *I knew his story was a lie*, he thought, laughing at himself for wasting time looking. He wandered around the grounds for another hour, looking at the crosses in the prison cemetery, poking his head into dozens of cells in the main building — the one they called the Asylum — and he left. If he ever needed another hideout, perhaps he'd come back here.

Ezekiel saw his friend not long after that and said the stairway didn't exist. The man replied that he'd missed it. He handed Ezekiel a key, told him what to do, and Ezekiel went back to try it out.

I'll be damned, he thought to himself as the shelf swung open. For once, his friend told the truth.

His flashlight came in handy as he walked down thirteen creaking stairs and entered a large room ringed by cells, each with a metal door that had a small barred window. Each one was only four feet square, too small for a man to lie down, and each one had a heavy metal ring — a shackle that would lock around a man's wrist — affixed to the back wall.

The ceiling was inches above his six-foot-three frame, and a heavy butcher-block table stood in the center of the room's concrete floor. This place reminded him of Dr. Frankenstein's laboratory, but this was no movie set. Awful things had gone on down here. Unspeakable things.

He examined the six-by-eight-foot sturdy wooden table. He saw four heavy iron cuffs, one on each corner, and a shallow, sloping groove ran from the middle of the table to one edge. Dark stains filled the groove, with more on the floor. The stains couldn't be what they looked like — blood, could they?

Why would a subterranean room have a huge butcher block in it? A slaughterhouse. That was it. The building above him had been a hotel kitchen. The cooks slaughtered animals and prepared cuts of meat on this table.

But why would a slaughterhouse need cells? Because someone had turned a prep room for the kitchen into a dungeon — solitary confinement. The Hole. They'd treated the inmates worse than animals, chaining them to the walls and forcing them to squat in a tiny room for hours — maybe days. He wondered if they'd given them food and water. It was a horrible place to imprison a human.

He wanted to ignore what he saw before him, but he couldn't sweep away the reality of what had happened here. Cooks didn't need iron cuffs to secure a lamb or a goat to the heavy table. Those restraints were for something else. They were for men. Prisoners had been spread-eagled on this table and … and he refused to consider what had happened after that.

He'd been around, but he had seen nothing like this. This was a scene from a horror movie, but it was real — a dungeon more awful than anything on film.

It was a place his friend would find interesting. The man said he stayed here sometimes, but that had to be another lie. No comfortable space existed in this place, not even for his strange friend.

A sound came from somewhere in the darkened room, startling him. He stood still, held his breath and listened.

There it was again!

There came a shuffling sound like someone dragging his feet as he walked.

Now a soft scraping noise came from somewhere behind him. He whirled about, playing the beam of his flashlight around the perimeter of the room.

He saw something he'd missed before. He thought every cell door was open, but across the room two doors were shut.

There came that sound again. Where did it come from? Perhaps from behind those closed doors?

Ezekiel couldn't recall the last time he'd felt real fear. Even when he was with his crazy friend, a guy who scared other people, he wasn't afraid. But it unnerved him being here in this horrific chamber, standing in a huge dark room with only a flashlight, knowing he was in a place where awful things happened. It would be easy to leave — to run back up the stairs. He'd be outside in seconds, away from this hellish place.

But he didn't run. Something drew him toward those two tiny rooms that lay behind metal doors. He rubbed the goosebumps on his arms, and he took a step, then another, until he stood before a cell.

He listened and then he reached for the door handle.

There was another muffled sound — a soft scratching noise — and now he realized it came from behind this door. Before fear overpowered him, he grabbed the handle and threw it open. The door swung better on its hinges than he expected, and it crashed against the wall just as an enormous black rat flew out of the room and disappeared into the darkness behind him. Startled and confused, he stumbled backwards and fell against the heavy table.

Recalling a movie from long ago, he half-expected the shackles to snap over his arms and legs, trapping him in a viselike grip. He recoiled and leapt off the table.

He went back to the cell. It differed from the others; it was larger — around eight by ten feet — and had no metal cuff. The walls looked different. Some kind of cloth had covered them once. The rats had done their work on it; batting and rodent droppings lay all over the floor.

In the back of the room lay a stone slab — perhaps once a bed — and a hole in the floor that once was a toilet.

Why was this room different? He ran his hand over the material on the walls, and he realized what it was — a padded cell. The Asylum's official name was Victory Institution for the Criminally Insane, and this place had been the worst part of the prison. He understood, and it surprised him there weren't more cells like this.

He heard something again — a much different noise, coming from the room next door. This wasn't a scratch or the scrape of a rat. It was terrible.

It was a moan. A long, melancholy sigh, part whisper, part groan.

He recoiled at the sound. He wanted out of here this instant, but without warning the cell door swung open, and a visible, opaque cloud of darkness, far blacker than the chamber itself, issued forth from the cell. Ezekiel cried out and raised his arms to ward off the cloud. He dropped the flashlight, and it rolled to a corner.

The blackness surrounded him like a heavy, oppressive blanket that pressed into his entire being. There came the sound again — that wretched sigh of sorrow, misery and suffering. Now the sound was here — all around him. Finding it hard to breathe, he panicked, sucking in gulps of air but needing more. About to lose consciousness, he turned, ran for the stairway, hyperventilated and passed out. He fell forward and collapsed on the floor, descending into a dreadful place inside his mind.

CHAPTER TWENTY-THREE

Where am I?

As his mind cleared, he stood, using the table to steady himself. He saw the flashlight's beam ten feet away, and he grabbed it. He recalled what had happened and the dark, angry clouds that had swarmed over him.

Both doors to the padded cells had been open earlier. An apparition — a frightening spirit — had floated through a cell door that opened by itself. How could it be closed again? The thing — if it was sufficiently corporeal to be called a thing — sucked the breath out of him. It had enveloped him as though it had hands and arms, touching his face, his body, his legs, and he'd collapsed into a nightmare of paralyzing terror.

He remembered a dream while he lay on the floor unconscious. A black mass of phantasms had whirled through his thoughts. They had to be fantasy, but they had been so bizarre and frightening that they seemed real.

The cloud that flew from the cell had been a mass of souls — the souls of prisoners, forgotten men who'd experienced this terrible room firsthand. Their moans and sighs were those of the lost, the damned, those with no hope.

He wanted to leave. As he ran across the room, there was another voice, a screeching scream.

Open the door to my cell.

Let me out, Ezekiel.

He flew up the stairs two at a time, unlocked the door, popped through into the pantry, and slammed the shelf closed. He sucked in air and forced himself to slow down so he wouldn't faint again.

After that experience, Ezekiel hoped he'd never visit that awful pit again, but June tenth was coming. His crazy friend looked forward to that special night, and you never knew what went on inside his head. Ezekiel never took part in the celebrations, but his friend bragged about the things he did. They might be more lies, but Ezekiel had an awful feeling his boasts were real.

CHAPTER TWENTY-FOUR

The best thing about this June tenth was that it fell on a Saturday. Saturday afternoon and Sunday were Landry's days off, so it was perfect.

Landry enjoyed his work at the *Daily Iberian*, but it was hard to focus as the time drew near. He had explained his project to Cate and gotten the permission he needed. That hadn't surprised him — she seemed as eager as he to learn what he might discover. It surprised him when she asked to come along. He enjoyed every minute with her, but this time he said no. Anything could happen; he even packed a pistol his dad gave him a long time ago. Disappointed, she gave up. "Just don't get yourself in trouble," she'd admonished him.

Landry was excited that Saturday morning. He hurried through his editing, and at last the Monday paper went to press. At home, he took out his list, double-checked the things lined up on his kitchen table, and walked through every step in his mind one last time. His mind raced with excitement and possibilities as he fidgeted and waited for the time to pass.

With the Jeep all packed, he couldn't kill any more time. He planned to be at the Asylum around seven p.m., but around five he parked the Jeep in the lot of the closed ShopRite market a mile from the Asylum. The weather forecast called for partly cloudy skies and an almost full moon. Arriving early turned out to be smart, he said to himself as dense, low-hanging storm clouds rolled in fast. Summer storms popped up in the humid evenings, and a rumble of thunder gave a preview of what to expect. Landry put on the poncho he'd brought just in case. Moonlight would have helped tonight, but he had to take whatever the weather gods dished out.

He hoisted a backpack, checked the pistol in his jacket pocket, and walked down the road that led to the Asylum. He would duck into the underbrush if a car approached, but this stretch of pavement only led to one place, a place most people avoided. Landry reached the arched entrance without seeing anyone — and without being seen.

Instead of walking up the main drive, he stayed out of sight in the trees. As he approached the old prison, a shiver ran down his spine. He wondered if he'd ever come here without being nervous. Ahead, the enormous building rose dark and forbidding, its corner turrets reaching to touch the ominous, low-hanging clouds. Now the wind was much stronger as it whipped through the tree limbs above him, moaning like the crazed inmates inside the Asylum might have moaned. He told himself to stop those thoughts. Tonight would be eerie enough without letting his mind dwell on ghost stories.

He picked a spot in the bushes offering a good view of the building. He rolled out a tarp and sat down, putting a thermos of coffee, some energy bars and his flashlight within reach. The sun set around seven thirty, and he felt an occasional raindrop. The wind howled and the trees swayed like banshees. He heard the scratching noises as they brushed against the walls of the building. He settled in to wait all night, probably for nothing. Nothing would be a good thing, because he hadn't planned what to do if something happened.

Since 1989, on or about June 10, fifteen people had died inside the building or on the grounds. Deaths hadn't happened every year, but the last ones were one year ago tonight. Those were the two homeless people, one stabbed to death in the cemetery and the other OD'd in the building.

Questions ran through his mind as the gray clouds, moving lower and lower, obscured the spires on top of the turrets. Should he have told someone besides Cate what he planned for tonight? Was he trying to prove something to himself — and to her — about his bravery? Was it crazy to tempt fate on the night so many awful things had happened?

At this point all that meant nothing. Here he sat all alone, getting colder by the minute and bracing for a thunderstorm.

He hid in the trees to watch the front and side windows and the entryway during the night that a murderer had struck over the years. The building was quiet; he didn't think there were trespassers tonight, and the only thing going on was the intensifying storm.

He saw something, perhaps a glimmer of light from the main road. With one hand on the gun, he watched and waited. It had been lightning in the distance, he decided. Nothing more.

Every so often he stood and stretched when his legs cramped. He listened for unusual sounds, but it was hard to hear with the wind screeching and the constant rumbles of thunder.

Around ten the rain started, quickly becoming a steady downpour. He hunkered down and pulled the brim of his cap low. The poncho worked well, but he wished he'd worn something besides his jeans, already wet and getting wetter by the minute.

He felt that something wasn't right. Nothing about the house or the grounds had changed, but something felt different.

Someone was nearby.

He drew the pistol, carefully turned, and looked behind him. A figure dressed in black stood in the trees ten feet away. He pointed the gun and tightened his grip.

"Landry! Stop!"

He lowered the pistol. "Cate! God, I might have shot you! Why did you sneak up on me?" He was angry at himself, but even more at her. He'd told her not to come, and by God, he might have shot her.

She wore a black slicker with the hood pulled down around her face. She sat on the tarp beside him and took off her backpack.

"I wasn't sneaking up on you," she snapped. "I didn't know where you were. I had no idea if you were even coming until I spotted your Jeep in the parking lot."

"Shh," he whispered. "Please don't shout. We agreed — "

"You agreed. You said I shouldn't come, and I agreed so you'd shut up. I want to learn what's going on here too. I have every right to be here. After all, this is my family's property. Let it go. Anything interesting going on?"

"Nothing. I've been here for hours, and there's nothing going on except a hell of a storm I didn't expect. I wish you hadn't come —"

"Thanks," she whispered with a grin. "I wish you weren't here either."

"That's not what I meant."

"Landry, it's your fault. You told me about all those unsolved cases and you got my attention. Thanks to Dad, I love mysteries, and I would not miss this one. I flew to Lafayette this afternoon, rented a car, and drove to your house to tell you I came to join you. You had already left, so I drove to Victory, parked beside the Jeep, and here I am, like it or not."

"I like it," he blurted. "I mean, sure, why not? It might be dangerous. That's what concerned me."

She laughed at his obvious discomfort. "All right, then. I'm glad that's settled." As the rain slowed and a light fog rolled in, she opened her pack and pulled out a thermos. "Hot cocoa?"

Now he laughed. "Are you ready for this? Did you leave Galveston expecting to sit outside for hours in the rain?"

"I left Galveston thinking this would be a warm June night, but once I realized the storm was coming, I ran by Walmart and picked up a thermos and this rain suit. Good thing I did!"

They shared hot chocolate and chatted for an hour. Without warning, she gripped his arm and pointed to the house. "Look at that!" she whispered.

Through the fog they saw something flicker in one of the building's windows. It was there for only a moment.

"There was a light on the road earlier," he said. "At least I thought so. I decided it was just the lightning."

"Look! There it is again! It's in the next window! That's no reflection!"

A light drifted across a fourth-floor window. It started on one side, and when it reached the other, it disappeared.

"Someone's up there," Cate whispered. "What do we do now?"

"Well, I guess we could find out who it is." This was the part Landry hadn't worked out. Although he'd hoped to learn something about the deaths at the Asylum, his sitting in the woods all night on June 10th couldn't explain anything.

She didn't understand why he hesitated. "You guess we could find out who it is? Isn't this why you wanted to stake out the house? You have proof something's going on in there. What's your plan now?"

"I didn't plan that part. I didn't expect to see anything, to be honest. Now I don't know what to do."

Surprised at his answer, she sat for several minutes without speaking. They had seen something, but the light hadn't reappeared and the windows were dark. It was a missed opportunity, but perhaps it was better not to confront whoever was in the house. It could be someone — or something — far more dangerous than a vagrant on drugs.

At last she spoke. "It's almost midnight. Nothing's happened for a long time. What should we do next?"

Embarrassed by his lack of prior planning, he knew he looked like a coward. He had a weapon he'd been trained to use, even if he had only fired it at the range. A deputy supposedly ready for trouble, here at a spooky house in a rainstorm with a girl he liked, Landry was afraid.

"It's best to go, given the weather," he said with false bravado. "You're liable to catch a cold."

Her eyes opened wide in surprise. "You're not going inside? You staked out the house, and you saw a mysterious light. Now you're just going to leave? You're not going to check it out?"

He spoke without thinking as words tumbled from his mouth. "I … I was talking about you leaving. It might be dangerous. Yes, I'm going in. That's what I'm here for, right? I want to see if I can find anything. I just think you might be afraid, and maybe it's better that you leave."

Liar, she thought. It was obvious he was making this up on the fly. "I came all the way from Galveston," she whispered. "I'm excited and scared too, but we have to know what's in there!"

She's something, Landry thought. *She's got backbone, and she's braver than I am.*

They folded the tarp, left it in the trees by his backpack, and stood on the edge of the yard as an enormous bolt of lightning tore through the sky and blasted a tree a hundred yards away, creating a deafening explosion.

"Shit!" Landry yelled as Cate grabbed his hand.

"That scared the hell out of me too! Come on. Let's get inside before we get struck ourselves!"

They abandoned the idea of being stealthy, raced to the porch, and darted through the yawning blackness into the Asylum.

The man who had watched them smiled. This was a special day. Until now he thought that like before, there would be no celebration this year. Then the young man came sneaking through the trees. The watcher was exhilarated. There would be a party this year after all!

It got even better when the girl showed up. That was a bonus. He was going to enjoy this June tenth very much. He had to lure them inside, but that ended up being no problem at all. He simply carried a lantern past a top-floor window.

BILL THOMPSON

Their curiosity got the best of them, and they came into the Asylum. Into his place.

Two of them, just like last year! How exciting!

CHAPTER TWENTY-FIVE

The cellphone rang five times before Sheriff Willie Barbour's wife jabbed him in the ribs and roused him awake. Not much happened at night in Iberia Parish on a Sunday night, but now and then there were things the deputies couldn't handle.

Willie glanced at his alarm clock. The dial flashed 10:30 p.m. and the date — Sunday, June 11. He fumbled for his phone, still clearing his head. He and his wife had gotten in bed early, and he had fallen asleep watching a rerun of *Miami Vice*. The late news was on now; he clicked it off with the remote as he answered.

"Sorry to bother you, Sheriff, but an alert came in a few minutes ago I thought you should know about. It's a BOLO for a girl from Galveston named Cate Adams."

A BOLO — the acronym for "be on the lookout" — meant the authorities were looking for a crime suspect.

"What's the big deal? What's so important about a BOLO you had to wake me up?"

"They're sending officers down from Baton Rouge, and I knew you'd want to be here when they arrived."

That got the sheriff's attention. He sat up in bed and looked for his socks. "Baton Rouge? The state's involved? What did she do, anyway?"

"She's missing, and there's something else you need to know. She was in the parish to see Landry Drake. Her father said she drove to New Iberia yesterday to meet him. She should have been home by noon today, but she never arrived."

Damn that Landry Drake! He gave me grief from the minute I met him, and here we go again.

He had to do something fast. Whatever was going on, it was a big deal because the state police were coming here. He had to show them he was on top of things in his parish.

He got Landry's home address from the deputy and said he'd check things out. Grumbling and muttering, he dressed and drove to the apartment house where Landry lived. The kid's Jeep wasn't in the parking lot. He banged on Landry's door over and over until the one next to it opened. A girl in her twenties stepped out. She recoiled when she saw an armed officer, and she hoped he didn't smell the joint she was holding behind her back.

"He's not home. He hasn't been home today."

"Do you know where he is?"

She didn't, so he drove to the office and issued an alert to his men patrolling the back roads of the parish. He pulled up the license number of Landry's Jeep and ordered them to look for it.

Half an hour later the radio crackled and a deputy in the field said, "Base, this is Unit Two. Sheriff Barbour, come in. Over."

"Barbour here."

FORGOTTEN MEN: THE BAYOU HAUNTINGS

"I found the Jeep, sir. It's in a parking lot in Victory. There's an Enterprise rental car next to it with Georgia plates."

Damn that kid! Those cold cases at the damned Asylum got him fired in the first place, and now he's out there with some missing girl!

The sheriff didn't intend to let the state cops make him look bad. He had to check things out before they arrived. He ordered the deputy back at the office to get on the horn to Enterprise while he got in his patrol car, flipped on the red lights and siren, and drove to Victory. Ten minutes later he pulled into the parking lot next to the two vehicles — Landry's Jeep and a late-model Chevy with a rental car sticker on the rear bumper. Soon the deputy radioed that the car was rented yesterday afternoon at the Lafayette airport by Cate Adams from Galveston, Texas. She should have returned it this morning.

Barbour had no idea who the girl was or what the pair was up to, but he had a hunch where they might be. He left a deputy with the cars and drove to the prison. He came up the long driveway still muddy from last night's drenching rain. In front of the main building, he checked his revolver, got a flashlight and walked in. He shouted Landry's name, but the only response was angry swoops from several bats near the ceiling.

The radio crackled; two state cops were waiting for him at the office. He left, having spent only a few minutes at the Asylum and doing no investigating, but at least he'd made the effort. That was something positive he could tell the big shots from Baton Rouge.

Sheriff Barbour and the men met for an hour. Harry Kanter, a lieutenant in his late fifties, did most of the talking.

"First time in my career I've ever gotten a call from the very top."

"The governor?" Barbour asked, surprised.

"Almost. My big boss is Colonel Talbot, superintendent of the state police. The call came from him straight to me. No chain of command, no nothing. Highly unusual. He ordered me and Sergeant English to get our asses down to New Iberia on the double and check things out. So tell me about this Landry Drake she came here to meet. Who is he?"

"He was my deputy for a little while, but...well, he fancied himself a detective like you, Lieutenant. Instead of following orders, he insisted on wasting time trying to solve thirty-year-old cold cases. I told him to back off, he ignored me, and when I caught him doing it again, I fired him. He works for the newspaper now. But enough about him. Who's the missing girl?"

The sergeant took a notebook from his pocket and consulted his notes. "Cate Adams is the daughter of a prominent doctor in Galveston. Yesterday, on Saturday, June 10, she flew to Lafayette and rented a car. Her father said she was coming here to meet Landry Drake. The father met Drake once — he came here, and the three of them spent a day together out on Bayou Teche. His daughter was due back this morning. When she didn't show up, he started the search.

"Cate told her dad she'd spend last night at the Holiday Inn and come home this morning. She never made it to the hotel, and she didn't return the rental car or make her flight. The father's got connections — he knows folks in high places. Even though it's Sunday, Dr. Adams spoke with the governor, the governor called the head of the Texas Rangers, and he called our boss, Colonel Talbot. The BOLO went out fast — way faster than normal — and here we are."

"I've located her car," the sheriff advised. "His too. They're parked side by side in a lot down in Victory, fifteen miles south of here. Once I got the BOLO, I alerted my deputies, and we found the cars."

"I've never heard of Victory. How did you locate the cars so fast?"

"It didn't surprise me to find his there. It's a long story, the reason why I fired Landry. Once my deputy found the cars, there was no doubt where they'd gone. I drove to an old building — a former prison. That place is where the cold cases happened that Landry wouldn't stop investigating."

He told them about the Asylum and Landry's hunch that he was close to finding something that would link a dozen cold cases. Then he told the lieutenant that the girl's story didn't add up. It sounded crazy that she'd spend money on a plane ticket, a hotel room and a rental car just to have dinner with Landry Drake, of all people.

"They're rich folks," Kanter replied. "All I can say is people with a lot of money sometimes do things we might consider crazy, because they can afford to and we can't. Let's run down to Victory."

While the state policemen followed the sheriff's patrol car, Lieutenant Kanter got an interesting piece of information. He wasn't sure how it would fit into the case, but it was significant.

Cate Adams's father owned the former mental institution.

The deputy who had guarded the cars headed home to sleep. The state cops lifted prints, took pictures, and then towed them to an impound lot in New Iberia, where investigators could continue the search for clues.

CHAPTER TWENTY-SIX

Landry and Cate crept into the building. His pistol in his hand, they took the stairs to the top floor and found the window where the light had been, in a hallway that led to the cellblock. Landry played his flashlight along the floor and saw boot prints.

She whispered, "At least it's not a ghost."

"That might have been better. Somebody's been in here. If it was kids, wouldn't they have stayed out of sight instead of calling attention to themselves? Whoever's here knew we were watching, and he tried to scare us off. I'll bet he thought we were teenagers who'd run away from a ghostly light in an abandoned building."

A gravelly voice from the darkness said, "What if he wanted to lure you inside?"

"Damn!" As Landry raised his pistol, a bright light blinded him. Someone had been in the room all along.

"I've got a gun on the girl! Drop yours or I'll kill her! Kick it across the room!"

The voice sounded raspy like a smoker's, but commanding. Landry obeyed.

"Girl, I'm tossing you a pair of handcuffs. Cuff his wrists behind his back."

Compliance was their only option. She did what he asked, and the man ordered Landry to sit on the floor. The light moved about the room for a moment, and Landry heard Cate utter a sigh, then there was something else — the sound of her body crumpling to the floor.

Landry tried to stand. He shouted, "What the hell did you do to her?"

"Sit down! She'll be asleep for a while, and I'd as soon kill you as not. Want to live a little longer, or call it even now? Either way's fine with me, since it's June tenth."

Those words frightened him. "Why are you doing this? People know we're here! They'll be looking for us."

"Sure they will. The oldest story in the book, kid. And I've heard 'em all."

The man had a strange, unique voice. Landry would recognize it if he heard it again even though he hadn't seen his captor's face. He waited, and when he sensed that the man was close, he fought with the only means he had. He lashed out with his foot but missed. A second later he felt a prick in his neck, then nothing at all.

———

Landry's head pounded as he emerged from his narcotic slumber. There was something — a muffled, familiar sound he thought he recognized.

He sat crouched on the floor in the darkness in a room so small he couldn't straighten his legs. One hand was free, but his other arm twisted above his head because his wrist was shackled to the wall. His arm cramped.

Where am I? How did I get here?

His body ached after being unconscious in a squatting position on the floor. The darkness was absolute. He stood, felt the walls, found a door, and located its handle and an open space in the middle with bars over it.

Landry understood where he was. This was a cell.

He recalled some of what had transpired. They went inside to investigate a moving light on the top floor. There was another person, and something happened — something he didn't remember. Now he was a prisoner.

He heard the sound again — a voice, her voice — nearby.

"Cate! Are you there?"

She sounded weak. "Yes! What happened? Where are we?"

"I think we're still in the Asylum, but I don't know what happened. My hand's cuffed to the wall."

Hers was too, and neither of them remembered how they got here. A veil had been drawn across their minds. He recalled one thing here and another there, but he couldn't connect them.

She was quiet for a moment, and then she said, "He's going to kill us."

Landry thought so too. He wanted to be brave for her, but he confessed his own fear.

Another piece of the puzzle clicked in his brain. "He drugged us. You fell to the floor, and then there was a pinprick in my neck. I came to a few minutes ago."

"I've been awake longer than you. I've been calling your name. I'm glad you're here." Her voice grew weaker. "I'm tired, Landry."

"We should try to stay awake. We have to get out of here!"

Cate didn't answer. Moments later, he succumbed too, falling into a deep, dreamless sleep.

He awoke with a start; he cried out as his arm twisted in its restraint. His shackled hand was numb; he stood and massaged his fingers until the circulation returned.

"Cate! Cate, can you hear me?"

"Yes. I fell asleep. I'm sorry."

"I can hear you too," the harsh voice said. The person was outside Landry's cell.

Something slid under his door. "Bread and water," the voice said. "You have five minutes to slide the tray back out." Another sliding sound came a moment later. She was nearby, maybe even next door.

"I need to go to the bathroom," Cate said.

"There's a hole in the corner."

"Why are you doing this to us? We meant no harm. What do you want from us?"

The voice sounded ecstatic. "Oh my, you wouldn't believe what I've got in store for you! I'll be back now and then. Ordinarily I'd take care of things tonight, it being June tenth and all, but since there are two of you, Sam and I need a little more time to decide what to do with you. Last year we had two, but it ended way too fast. We may keep you a few days this time. We want to savor the experience!"

When he had gone, Landry squatted while frightening things invaded his thoughts. He'd fallen into a trap — they had been lured into the Asylum on June tenth. Two people died here last year, and the man holding them captive was the murderer. June tenth was important to him. They would die next.

She sobbed, and tears rolled down his cheeks too. He could think of nothing to say to comfort her.

Thanks to my taking unnecessary risks, he has us where he wants us.

They were his next victims, and it sounded as though he couldn't wait to get started.

Either they escaped, or they would die very soon.

All this was his fault. He should have listened to the sheriff and dropped his investigation of the strange events at the Asylum. He damned sure shouldn't have come here at night on June tenth. Coming alone was stupid enough, but then she showed up. It was her decision, he told himself, but he was to blame.

He hoped the cops would look for them. He was due at work on Monday the twelfth. Was it Monday already? Would his editor call the sheriff? If he did, what would the sheriff do? Would someone find his Jeep and call the cops? He had questions, but no answers.

Cate's father was their best hope. She said he knew almost everything about her trip. Her only fib was saying she went to New Iberia for dinner with Landry. Regardless, when she didn't make her flight home on Sunday and she didn't answer her phone, he'd act quickly. Perhaps that was already happening. He prayed it was.

CHAPTER TWENTY-SEVEN

Landry heard muffled voices and recognized a word now and then. Two men were talking. He recognized one — the grating voice of their kidnapper. The other voice, much harder to hear, sounded familiar. He struggled to remember why, but his addled brain didn't cooperate. The man had said he and Sam would decide what to do with them. The other voice must be Sam's, whoever he was.

Now they argued. The quieter voice said, "We can't...too dangerous...different than the others...holding them long-term...too risky...people will be looking."

The harsh one laughed. "...worry too much...only a few days...can't pass up two for one...fun."

The other person wasn't buying it. "I don't...we can't..."

Time was running out and Landry had to get free. He checked his shackle; it had been in the wall since before the Asylum closed in 1907. Over a hundred years old, it wasn't as secure as it had been. In the darkness, he ran his fingers over everything. Two chain links connected the shackle to a metal plate, and four bolts held the plate to the wall. The plate moved when he tugged to the right and left, and he spent the next hour rocking the shackle back and forth, back and forth until one bolt popped out.

Although his wrist bled, he kept tugging until a second bolt broke free. Now one side of the plate was loose, and he could pry with his good hand. In a few minutes the other bolts snapped. He was exhausted, and his hand remained cuffed, but he was free.

The simple part was over — now he had to figure out how they could escape from wherever they were. He got a break when he pushed on his cell door. Unlocked, it swung open.

"Cate? Where are you?"

She sighed, as though even speaking was a struggle now. "What do you mean, where am I? I'm here with you."

"Whisper. I'm free. Keep talking so I can find you." He found her cell, opened the door, and she hugged him with her free arm.

"Don't leave me! I don't know how you got away, but don't leave me!"

Her cuff was secure, just as his had been. He told her his plan — weak, but all he had — and she understood he had to leave, but he'd be nearby.

He sneaked into the main room, stood in one corner and waited.

He saw the light before he heard the man coming. A dim glow arose from one of the back cells, growing brighter as the man stepped through the metal door and into the room. He wore a hat pulled down low that hid his face. He balanced two trays in one hand and held the flashlight in the other. The man walked to Landry's cell and bent down to push the tray under the door. As he stood and shined his light through the tiny window in the cell door, Landry made his move.

Landry didn't know if his assailant was young or old, fit or flabby, a pugilist or a sissy. He wasn't a fighter, but with only one chance, he ran across the room. As the man turned, Landry swung the shackle. He aimed for the head, but the plate struck his arm with a glancing blow instead. The second tray and the flashlight fell to the ground as their kidnapper grunted, turned and ran.

Landry took the light and looked around, but he vanished, perhaps from where he'd come in. Nothing mattered now but escaping. He ran to Cate, opened the door and told her what he'd done. He shined the light on her restraint, desperate for some fast solution, and he saw something he'd missed.

A ring holding two keys was hooked to the bottom of the flashlight.

He tried them, one worked, and now she was free. Soon he was too. He shined the light around the large room, seeing for the first time that all four sides had cells, and there was a large heavy table in the middle.

On the far wall he saw a stairway. They hurried up thirteen stairs; at the top was a solid wall. He ran his hand over smooth wood.

"This has to be the way out. We have to open this!"

"Did you hear the men talking earlier?" she asked. "I did, and I couldn't have heard them through the wall, right? There has to be another way out."

"There is. The guy came from somewhere at the back of that big room, but we can't go where he is. This is our only chance!"

They had to get past this wall. He searched every seam, every seal on all four sides. Then from somewhere below came a cruel laugh and that unmistakable voice.

"You've made a mistake. That's the wrong way. You wouldn't want to miss the party!"

They were trapped at the top of the stairs.

"Look down there! What's that?"

She pointed to a small hole near the bottom of the door. He knelt and looked into a tiny keyhole. He inserted the smaller key, turned it, and the solid wall swung open.

They emerged into a pantry about ten feet square with a door on the opposite wall. Hearing footsteps on the stairs, Landry slammed the door, found a matching keyhole on this side, and locked it.

The solid wall they'd encountered was the back of an empty floor-to-ceiling row of storage shelves. It was cleverly concealed; if a person didn't know it was there, he would never have suspected it hid a staircase.

"We have to get out of here fast. Like I said, there's another way into that chamber. If he can get to the outside a different way, he'll find us fast."

He opened the pantry door, and they stepped into an unfamiliar hallway. Everything was still as they raced down the hall and entered a large room where sunlight streamed through floor-to-ceiling windows. After all that time in the dark, it took a moment for their eyes to adjust. They were in an old kitchen. Three rusty cast-iron stoves, several sinks and two large wooden iceboxes were covered by a thick layer of dust. This was an ancient, commercial kitchen from the days before modern appliances.

She pointed out the window. "Look! It's the Asylum! We're in the old kitchen!" They were two hundred yards behind the main building.

"Run!" he said, grabbing her hand. They raced across the broad yard and around the building, heading for where they'd left the cars and staying close to the trees by the road in case he came after them. They came to the intersection of Iberia Road and Main Street and darted into the parking lot, but the cars were gone.

She screamed, "What do we do now? We have to get away from here! This is the only road out. They'll be coming for us!"

"Nobody lives in town, but there are farms a mile or so from here. They'll have a phone. Let's go!"

"How? We can't just walk down the road in the open!"

At that moment, their luck took a turn. They heard a truck approaching. Landry stayed out of sight until he could see it, then stepped to the pavement and waved. The UPS driver pulled up alongside him, heard his story, and agreed to break company policy. No riders were allowed in UPS trucks, but he drove them to the first house they saw, where he had a drop-off anyway, and Landry called his old boss, Sheriff Barbour.

CHAPTER TWENTY-EIGHT

After Landry's call, things happened fast.

Three hours after their escape, cops combed the main building, going floor by floor and room by room. The detritus of those who had passed through — discarded clothes, rubbish, needles, graffiti and human waste — was everywhere, but no one was around.

Lieutenant Kanter asked Cate and Landry to stay in his sedan while a second team went through the kitchen outbuilding. One of his men stayed with them since the kidnapper was still unaccounted for.

"Why would they have put cells under the kitchen?" he asked as they waited.

"The room's been there since the hotel was built. I showed it to you on Dad's plans, but we didn't go there. Dad never took me there either. Remember, I told you Dad thought they might have demolished it to keep prisoners from escaping there. It was a larder in the old days — a dark, cool place to store meat, beer and wine for hotel guests. Once it became a prison, somebody had the idea to…to do something bad down there."

He wondered why they had a secret entrance and a hidden stairway. "It was a torture chamber," he said, "with all those cramped cells and manacles on the walls."

"I think so too," she whispered. "I'll bet that's where they dealt with the bad ones."

They sat in silence, and he pondered what horrific things had happened down there.

The cops finished with the kitchen, and Lieutenant Kanter brought them inside. Landry showed them how to open the secret wall, and they waited in the kitchen while four state policemen, tactical vests on and weapons drawn, went down the narrow stairway.

They heard a muffled shout that meant the officers were in the chamber.

"POLICE! FREEZE!"

Fifteen minutes later the men came upstairs, and everyone gathered in the kitchen to hear their report. They described the room, with cells along its perimeter and a heavy table in the middle just as Landry and Cate had said. The basement was empty; the one Landry struck in the arm and the other one — the quiet one called Sam — were gone.

"At least one of them was there when we escaped," Landry had told them earlier. "I heard the raspy voice when we were on the stairway trying to open the door. When I was hiding in the room before that, I saw his light come from somewhere in the back. They went out a different way."

The cops didn't see a second exit, and Kanter apologized for asking them to do something critical.

"I can't force you to do this, and I know it'll be hard, but I hope you'll go down there and tell me what we're missing.

My men will go ahead of you, and you'll wear vests. Can you do it?"

Cate squeezed his hand and nodded. He did too, and soon they went down the stairway into the musty room where five armed state policemen guarded the perimeter of the chamber. Thanks to a lot of flashlights, they could at last see what had been their prison.

Kanter said it looked like a medieval torture chamber.

Cate told the cop that the floor plans showed this room and a similar one below the main building, connected by what might be an underground tunnel. Earlier they thought the rooms no longer existed. Maybe the secret staircase wasn't secret back then, she suggested. Maybe you walked through the pantry and down the stairs.

Landry had thoughts too. "I think when they built the prison, this room was the Hole. They stuck the worst of the worst down here and chained them to the walls. The guards did whatever they wanted to the ones who ended up here. They hid the stairs behind a set of shelves in the pantry, they built all these tiny cells, and they installed this table for something awful. This room was ideal for their purposes. It's a long way from the cellblocks, and nobody outside could hear the screaming."

As he described the horrors, there came a sepulchral wail — an eerie sound that began so softly they didn't notice it, but intensified like the wind before an approaching storm until it descended like a blanket around them.

Everyone looked around in alarm. The cops struck at the darkness with their weapons, but there was nothing to hit. Landry took out his phone and began to video.

Even the detective, a former Marine who'd served two tours in Iraq, shuddered. "What the hell was that?" Kanter muttered, glancing around the room and ordering his men to search the cells again. They found nothing as Landry knew they wouldn't.

"It's the forgotten men," Cate murmured. "They're trapped here."

Whoever — whatever — had made that sound might have been human once, but none of them had ever heard such a plaintive cry. It was despondent and lost.

Kanter said, "Whatever's going on here has a rational explanation. There's no such thing as a haunted building, and I damned sure don't believe in ghosts. Landry, let's see if we can find that other entrance where you saw the light."

Now from across the room a thin, filmy cloud wafted from a cell. Seeing it, a cop yelled in alarm.

"Something just touched me!" another shouted.

His partner beside him laughed, but his laughter turned to fear as he saw something in the air. It had been wispy, but it was rapidly becoming a black, semitransparent shape.

"What the hell is that?" he asked, backing away from it.

Landry knew. "It's them. Their souls can't leave this place."

Cate drew back, but he told her not to be afraid. "I don't think they'll hurt us. I think they want to be free."

In seconds, the cloud dissipated into nothingness, and Landry, who'd been unconsciously holding his breath, exhaled at last.

"Are you okay?" she asked, touching his sleeve.

"Yeah. I got spooked, that's all."

Each of them, cops included, was unnerved by what just happened. Getting back to business, Kanter asked Landry which cell could have been the one where he'd seen the light. Landry pointed to a few, and the cops got to work.

"Lieutenant! Come take a look over here!"

Kanter walked to the cell where his man was on his knees examining its back wall.

"Sir, this wall's different from the other cells. I can trace a rectangle — do you see it?" He moved his finger along a faint groove running from the floor up one side for about five feet, then across the top and back down again. "It might be another hidden door."

As the cop looked for another keyhole like the one in the pantry, Landry said this likely was the way their captor came and went. Maybe it was from somewhere behind that wall that they'd heard two men arguing. Maybe their kidnapper came and went through here.

Three men crammed inside the tiny cell, one holding a light while the other two ran their hands over every inch of the wall. Then one found a recessed switch and yelled, "Got it!"

The cops stepped out of the cell so their boss could see. He looked into a passageway leading off into the darkness, a hallway that had been hidden behind another false wall. He ordered two men to check it out.

Weapons drawn, the men bent and walked through a five-foot-high, three-foot-wide corridor that had been dug through the earth. Kanter kept his light trained on them until they made a turn and went out of sight.

In a moment they heard, "Holy shit! What the hell's this about?"

"You okay?" Kanter shouted, and someone said yes. Five minutes later they returned.

"There's no one there," one said.

The other one added, "Well, there's a man in there, sitting in a chair."

Confused, Kanter snapped, "So is there someone there? Did you restrain him?"

"Not necessary, sir. There's a whole living area set up in there. Furniture, an ice chest, a kitchen table and chairs. It's like a bizarre one-room house."

The other cop jumped in. "And there's a body sitting in a recliner. A corpse, sir. He's wearing clothes, shoes, everything, but he's been dead a really long time. He's dried out, like one of those dried-apple dolls, and there's gray stuff — maybe mold — all over his skin. Oh, one more thing. His clothes are prison issue."

"What the hell are you talking about?" Kanter said. "Are you sure?"

"Go see for yourself, sir. It's bizarre, I know, but he's in there all right."

Kanter went down the corridor, came back in a few minutes, and took Cate and Landry into the strange place. Bizarre was a good description, Landry thought as he looked at the dirt walls, floors and seven-foot ceiling, into which a twelve-foot-square space had been carved that looked surprisingly like a studio apartment.

It was neat and tidy. Flatware, dishes and glasses were set for two persons at a kitchen table covered with a gingham cloth. A cot was in one corner, all made up with sheets, a blanket and two fluffy pillows. There were two recliners. An ashtray sat on a small table next to one, a pipe and smoker's tools resting inside, all ready for the occupant's next relaxing smoke.

In the other recliner sat the corpse.

Kanter instructed everyone to stay away from the body until the medical examiner could come. From across the room, Landry and Cate looked at the strange figure. The word *INMATE* was stenciled on the front of his orange shirt, and the same word ran down one leg of his matching orange pants. He wore a black ball cap and tattered sneakers.

"Look at his fingernails," Cate said with a shiver. "My God, they must be six inches long. Think they kept growing after he died?"

Kanter shook his head. "Skin pulls back as it putrefies. The nails are the same length as before, but they look longer because of that."

Landry shook his head in amazement. "This is crazy. What do you think, Lieutenant?"

"The ME will get DNA samples to find out who he was. Offhand, I'd guess he escaped from prison a long time ago, somehow ended up here, built himself a hideaway, and sat down and died in that chair."

"But why would he have his prison uniform?" she asked. "The first thing I'd do is get rid of them. He spent some time building this place and stocking it with food. You'd think the clothes would have been the first thing to go."

Kanter nodded. "Maybe he didn't build it. What if someone on the outside helped him escape and brought him here, where a secret place had been made ready for him? Maybe he got a knock on the head during the escape somehow, and he died shortly afterwards."

A week later, the medical examiner provided a cause and approximate date of death. He also took DNA from the corpse, but he had nothing to match it with. The unknown white male, about thirty-three years of age, had died in November or December 1988 from blunt-force trauma to the back of the skull.

Someone had bashed in his head and put him in a recliner.

CHAPTER TWENTY-NINE

Landry and Cate met Lieutenant Kanter at Starbucks. They hadn't seen him in almost two weeks and were eager to hear what new things he'd turned up.

Kanter said his men searched for relatives of the prison escapees to perform DNA testing. All three men were born and raised in rural Iberia Parish, and relatives still lived in the area. They located Samuel Gold's aging mother and the brother of Thomas Small, and both provided DNA samples. Mackey Thorn, the third escapee, had no living relatives. The elderly grandparents who raised him died years ago.

Kanter said, "The corpse in the recliner is Samuel Gold. As you know, the cops presumed they recovered his body from the lake in 1989.

"The ME estimated Gold died in November or December 1988. He escaped Angola on November 20, and if the ME's date is right, he died within forty days. He wore prison clothes, indicating he died soon after the escape. Did he have an accident, or was he murdered? If he was, did one of the others do it? If so, why kill him right after they escaped?"

He paused for a sip of coffee, and Landry said, "Have they exhumed the three bodies from the pickup in the lake?"

"No. The DA filed a request, but the judge hasn't acted on it yet. As you know, the bodies weren't actually identified. Everyone made assumptions, but now we know Sam Gold wasn't in the pickup."

"Where are they buried?" Cate asked.

"No one claimed the bodies, so the state paid for a pine box and an interment. Their graves are in the back of the local cemetery — no headstones, just wooden crosses, from what I'm told. Once the judge allows the exhumation, I hope we can learn their identities."

Landry asked, "What's your professional opinion at this point? Are two of the three guys the other escaped convicts?"

"I'm not sure, but after all these years without a sighting or a word, I believe all three are dead. Whether they're the bodies from the lake, the ME's report will tell us. I'll say this. If they're alive, I'm amazed they stayed free for all these years."

Cate asked if Kanter was still trying to find relatives of the third convict, Mack Thorn.

"No. When I get time, I'll work on it again. I heard he got married when he was a teenager, back before he went to Angola. The only shot we have is if there was a child to provide the DNA sample we need."

Landry asked Thorn's wife's maiden name.

"Susanna. Susanna Copeland."

Susanna Copeland. The name was vaguely familiar, but Landry couldn't remember why.

The next morning, Landry ran the parish's public records database and found four entries for a Susanna Copeland. It was so simple that he wondered why the detective hadn't taken five minutes to look. But Kanter was trying to learn who the corpse was, not to find an escapee who died thirty years ago.

He jotted down the facts.

In June 1975, Susanna Copeland and Mackey Thorn, both eighteen, married.

In 1978, a year after Mack went to prison, Susanna Copeland Thorn filed for divorce on grounds of cruelty, and Mack didn't contest it.

Two days after her divorce was final, Susanna Copeland — she now dropped her despicable husband's last name — married James Christian Romero, attorney at law.

In 1991, someone killed them in their bedroom. Landry had seen that case in the database, and that was why her name was familiar.

He did more digging in the newspaper's archives for anything about Mackey Thorn and turned up more than he'd expected. Mack was violent even as a youth and went to reform school at fifteen.

Mad Mack's ex-wife couldn't help them because she'd been dead for twenty years. Did they have a child? Landry searched the vital records registry for the last name Thorn in the late seventies, but he found nothing.

He read his notes once and then another time. Something was missing, and now he saw it. Why hadn't he figured this out earlier? It was as clear as day.

He knew why unsolved murders had happened at the Asylum for the last thirty years.

He knew who had committed them.

He knew how a common date linked them, and who had kidnapped Cate and him at the Asylum.

Now everything made sense.

BILL THOMPSON

CHAPTER THIRTY

"I figured out what happened," Landry began when Lieutenant Kanter answered his call. The detective turned on his recorder; if Landry had solved the mystery, Kanter couldn't miss a word.

Landry reminded the detective he had searched the parish database for crimes at the Asylum. Online records only went back to 1980. From 1980 until the year Mack escaped in 1988, there were no reported crimes at the prison. Starting on June 10, 1989, and continuing for the next twenty-eight years, at least thirteen people had died on or around that date, all at the Asylum.

"Why do you say 'at least thirteen'? Do you think there are more?"

"Yes. At least four more that fit the pattern."

"Interesting. Tell me about those."

"Last year two people died out there on June tenth. They'd spent at least one night there, maybe more, and the sheriff's department called it a drug-induced murder-suicide. Someone killed the girl in the cemetery, and the guy died inside the building from an overdose. He killed her, went back inside, and killed himself, or so they concluded. Case closed."

"Why do you think that decision was wrong?"

"Because it happened on June tenth. It all makes sense because of the last piece of the puzzle. There was one more crime. On June 10, 1991, Susanna and James Romero were murdered in his townhouse in New Iberia. Do you recall that crime?"

Kanter perked up. "Sure. I think it was the only double murder in parish history."

"I found out the dead woman's last name. It was Copeland. The lawyer's wife was Susanna Copeland."

"Mack Thorn's ex-wife."

"Right. And her husband was Mack's attorney when he got life in prison at Angola. Mack thought he should have done better. Mack hated him for that, and then his wife divorced him and married Romero two days later. How do you think that made Mad Mack react?"

"You're telling me you think Mack Thorn is still around, committing crimes on June tenth every few years?"

"I'm certain, and here's why. June tenth was his wedding anniversary. He and Susanna were eighteen when they married on June 10, 1975. He'd just finished a three-year stint in reform school, but since juvenile records are sealed, I can't see what crime he committed. Regardless, he got out, married Susanna, and kept on being his charming self.

"He beat his grandfather half to death — charges were filed but dropped when nobody would testify against him. When he was twenty-one, he raped and killed a girl in Lafayette. That got him sent to Angola for life at age twenty-two. I can't imagine how relieved his wife must have been. She was just a kid when she married him, and I'll bet she was enamored with his wild life, but I also bet he mistreated her. It was just who he was. Once she was confident he was gone for good, she divorced him and he was furious. He kept that hatred festering for years and then he broke out. Mack killed her and the lawyer on his and Susanna's wedding anniversary."

Impressed by his deductions, Kanter joked that Landry should become an investigative reporter. Landry laughed, saying he'd have to move. In a sleepy town like New Iberia, he'd starve to death for lack of things to investigate.

"I'm going to call the judge and get those bodies exhumed quickly," the detective said. "We have to know who died in that pickup thirty years ago. From what you've told me, I'm thinking none of them were the escapees."

There was more, Landry said. He revealed his fruitless search for a possible child of Mack's, but while they were talking, he realized he'd missed a step. He'd limited his online search to Iberia Parish. What if Mack had a child who was born somewhere else?

Later, Landry did a statewide search and called Kanter again. "They had a child, a girl stillborn in February, 1976 in a hospital in Lafayette, where Susanna was from. I should have checked that earlier."

"Do you know where she's buried?"

"You called me an investigative reporter — remember? I investigated. The child's buried in Calvary Cemetery in Lafayette. I drove up and found her grave." He texted a picture of the marker. "It's a simple carved stone, and from the inscription, I'd say Susanna's parents paid for it."

"That doesn't surprise me," Kanter said as he looked at the picture. "I don't see Mack as a compassionate father."

The stone bore a carving of a lamb and the words *Baby Girl Thorn. Stillborn February 5, 1976. Our granddaughter is in the arms of Jesus.*

"Good work," the detective told Landry. "This is exactly what I need. I'll see if I can locate Susanna's parents. If they'll allow us to exhume the body, we'll have the DNA we need."

It took a month for everything to fall into place, but at last the exhumation orders came through. When the bodies were disinterred, the authorities learned more about three men who were pulled from a pickup at Lake Fausse Pointe in 1989. That was the good news. The bad news was only one could be identified.

Thomas Small, the rapist who escaped with Mack and Sam, was in the truck. The identities of the others remained a mystery. For years, the cops had believed they were Gold and Thorn, but Sam Gold was a desiccated corpse sitting in a recliner at the Asylum. And Mack's daughter's DNA proved the third body in the truck wasn't his.

Kanter revealed the autopsy results after telling Landry he couldn't tell anyone until the ME released his findings. Once Landry heard, he had an idea. If he could locate Mack Thorn and alert the police, he'd be able to write his own ticket. Maybe he really could become an investigative reporter at a large metropolitan newspaper in Atlanta or Miami — anywhere sounded more exciting than New Iberia.

Landry was on his own. Neither Kanter nor Cate would have condoned his plan, so he didn't tell them. It wouldn't be easy, but nothing important was ever easy. He would lie low, stay hidden, and keep his phone handy. If everything went as planned, Mack Thorn would show up, the cops would swoop in, and it would all be over. If anything went wrong, all he had to do was leave.

He went over things in his mind so many times they seemed straightforward and simple.

It's strange how a person can convince himself everything will go well when he wants something enough.

He made a list of what he would take on the stakeout.

The hardest thing was his job. He spoke with Ty Jones, his boss at the newspaper, explaining that he had personal business to attend to. He needed a few days off — how many, he couldn't say.

Landry had two strikes against him. He was a temporary employee, and he hadn't been on the job long enough to get time off. Jones was nice enough, but he told Landry if he had to be away, there was no choice but to fire him.

"You promised to stay," Jones said as he walked Landry to the door. "Thanks to you I'm in a jam, but you've done a good job. You have a future, but not unless you do what you say you'll do. Come back and see me when you're ready to commit. No promises; we'll talk then."

You also have to have faith in your convictions, Landry thought to himself as he walked away from the second job he'd ever had. It wasn't a permanent job anyway, he rationalized, and maybe the paper would still need a temp when this was over. If he was lucky, it might not be that long. If he wasn't lucky, he might never be back.

He dismissed the thought. He had to stay positive about all this and not lose his focus. This was a mission to solve a mystery.

Landry reconnoitered the grounds to find the best spot. He needed to observe not only the Asylum, but the kitchen where Mack had his secret underground room.

Landry was certain Mack would come back to the place he'd lived for thirty years. Now the police were gone and the Asylum was quiet, so he'd be back soon. There could be two people — he and Cate had heard two voices — so he had to be twice as careful.

He spread out a blanket in a thicket two hundred yards from the main building. He had a clear view of the back and one side, and he could also see the old kitchen fifty yards away. The ancient prison cemetery was to his left, its crosses hidden by tall oak trees that swayed in the morning breeze.

Settling in for what could be a long wait, he arranged his bottle of water, muted iPhone and granola bars. He fished his tablet from his backpack and started a novel about ghosts in Cajun country. It seemed appropriate since he was sitting in the shadows of the most haunted building in the state.

He would stay for as long as it took, coming here every day until he saw someone. But he really didn't have long to wait at all.

CHAPTER THIRTY-ONE

Reverend Ezekiel Billings was getting tired. He'd been at this evangelical stuff a long, long time, and his booming voice, his commanding presence, and his swashbuckling ability to sway sinners to salvation were feeling the test of time.

Only four people had responded to his fervent invitation to find Christ this evening at the Ebenezer Emmanuel Pentecostal Church in Sunset. And three were children. They were the most susceptible, more easily caught up in Ezekiel's tales of the danger of ignoring God's call.

What if you died tonight? It can happen, my friends! No one knows when his time is up, and do you want to be meeting St. Peter himself at the pearly gates, or do you want to face Satan in the fiery pit of Hell for the rest of eternity?

The timeworn lines had worked before, but he didn't feel like putting as much enthusiasm into the delivery as he used to do. The words were the same, but the fire-and-brimstone part had been lacking tonight. He didn't feel up to it.

Ezekiel lay in a feather bed under a down comforter, feeling much older than his sixty-three years. He was in the Johnson's guest bedroom, to which he had retired after picking at the chicken and dumplings Sister Johnson had so lovingly prepared.

He hadn't felt right since that day when he'd found the chamber hidden beneath the kitchen at the Asylum. He'd had some kind of epiphany down there — some kind of sign from...well, he wasn't sure exactly who. It wasn't God; he was certain of that. For a man who preached God's word and had memorized half the Bible, he knew for a fact God wouldn't be wasting time on Ezekiel Billings. What Ezekiel had done would be repugnant even to himself if he had a conscience like other people. Which he didn't.

Now things were catching up with him. He didn't know how much longer he could keep up the masquerade that he'd performed for all these years. The thing that always worried him in the past — succumbing to the desires of the flesh and getting Sister Whoever pregnant — wasn't the issue anymore. His sexual cravings — and those other cravings he suppressed so often — were on the wane. He worried about slipping up, making a mistake, and revealing something that could get him into serious trouble. His mind wasn't clicking like it once had. It was harder to focus nowadays. Just this evening, his thoughts had drifted as he sat on the dais at the two-bit country church where he was holding a revival. And last week the preacher had to call his name twice before he snapped back into reality and strode to the pulpit to deliver his message.

He wasn't himself these days. He couldn't risk another mistake. It was time to hang it up, but where would he go? What would he do?

Sleep came in short bursts that night, filled with disturbing dreams with frightening scenarios where he was suffocating — literally drowning — in a heavy blanket of terrible, overpowering memories.

Two weeks later he made his decision. He'd return to the cabin on the island, the place where that doctor from Galveston had run him off. He had kept an eye on it — nobody ever came around, and if the owner returned, the worst he could do was kick him out again. In the meantime, Ezekiel could relax and unwind, all by himself, which suited him just fine.

Ezekiel chose a three-night stand in Charenton for his grand finale. At somewhere around three thousand residents, it was larger than many of his stops, and maybe the people would be generous with their love offerings for the retiring evangelist.

He felt good about the decision he'd made. On the first night of his last revival, as he stood in front of nearly two hundred people seated in folding chairs inside a tent, he was exhilarated. His mind was as sharp as ever, he felt connected to the people as he preached from the book of Matthew, and a few of the women wept as he spoke of the peril of dying unsaved. That hadn't happened in a long time, and he was genuinely moved, as much as a man like Ezekiel Billings could be genuinely anything.

He'd just gotten to the best part — the place where he wove the words into a crescendo and had people on the edge of their seats — when there came a commotion from the back of the tent as two state policemen walked in with pistols drawn.

Pastor Burns jumped from his chair behind Ezekiel and shouted, "What's the meaning of this? This is the house of God!"

The cops moved down the aisle, guns pointed at the podium where the evangelist stood, a blank look on his face as they advanced toward him.

One yelled, "Mackey Thorn, you're under arrest for capital murder. Put your hands up!"

For a second, Reverend Billings stood transfixed, apparently not understanding. Mack was here, all right, but not inside the tent. What was going on here? He slowly raised both hands to the sky, one still clutching the Bible he'd been preaching from seconds earlier. Eyewitnesses later would argue whether the raised hands were an act of resignation or defiance.

Whatever the evangelist was thinking, the man who'd brought him here came to his rescue.

Pastor Burns shouted to the crowd that this was a terrible mistake. "Our beloved man of God is in danger," he screamed, and the people went berserk. There was pandemonium and mass confusion in the tent. Mack Thorn's name was familiar to everyone from all the recent publicity. People knew the violent criminal was still at large. But they also knew Reverend Billings wasn't him. Ezekiel Billings was a preacher, not a murderer. He'd been doing revivals for years.

"Help Reverend Billings!" came the cries from his followers. People jumped up from their seats, a few ran for the exits, but most crowded the aisles to protect the preacher. They stood firm and locked arms so the cops couldn't advance. In all the confusion, the police were forced to lower their weapons to avoid accidentally shooting someone. And they lost sight of their target.

At last the policemen snaked through the crowd, but when they reached the dais, he wasn't there. They screamed at Pastor Burns, asking where Billings was. The poor minister didn't know what to do or who to believe. He pointed to a flap at the back of the tent. The officers raced through it and emerged into a sea of vehicles, a field out back where two hundred people had parked their pickups in no particular order. In this mess, it was impossible to see if anyone was out there.

They searched, but they knew it was useless. Reverend Billings was gone.

CHAPTER THIRTY-TWO

Billings darted through the back flap of the tent and met up with Mack, who had been waiting for him as usual. They stayed low, zigzagging through the parked vehicles and ignoring the riot that was unfolding in the tent behind them. Ezekiel fled for his life, running as fast as his sixty-three-year-old legs would allow, and his old friend stayed right with him. They ran through town, avoiding the main streets and staying far from the lights. The moon guided them eastward towards Bayou Teche two miles away.

"I'll never get away," Billings huffed as he struggled to maintain the pace. "I can't keep up!"

"So you're just going to quit?" Mack wheezed. He was as old as Ezekiel and in just as bad shape, but he had the grit and determination that came from years in prison. "I guess it's up to me to get your ass out of trouble! Come on!"

By the time they reached the shoreline, they could hear sirens. They had to hurry. Several small boats bobbed in the water, and Mack knew from experience that people around here were careless about locking their things. It took only a few minutes to find a rickety bass boat with the key still in the motor. They jumped in, Mack started it up, cast off, and headed north up the bayou. They were going somewhere safe, he told Ezekiel, back to the cabin at Lafitte Landing. From there he'd figure everything out. He was the smart one about these things, not this Bible-thumping preacher.

Mack guided the boat around to the back side of the island where anyone coming up the bayou wouldn't see it. Ezekiel's heart pounded from exhaustion and adrenalin as he helped Mack pull the boat into some brush along the shore. He did his best, but he wasn't feeling good at all. The tension, the two-mile dead run to the bayou, the constant fear they'd capture him — all of it gave him palpitations and made him take breaths in deep gasps. They went through the trees on an unfamiliar path; neither had been on that side of the small island before. It didn't help that the moonlight that had guided them to the bayou was now obscured by dense forest. It was so dark they could see only a foot or so ahead of them. Without a flashlight, they used their outstretched arms to push through the brush.

The cabin was roughly in the middle of the woods, and soon they emerged into the clearing where it stood bathed in moonlight. Ezekiel was having problems breathing, huffing and puffing to get oxygen. He collapsed on the porch and lay there in pain. In all these years, this was the only time they had been close to being caught, and he had been unprepared for the sense of panic that had swept over him.

Exhausted too, Mack stretched out next to his old friend and tried to catch his breath. How had the cops figured it out? They had been so careful. Ever since they'd kidnapped that guy and girl, everything had gone to hell.

After that episode, Mack couldn't go back to the Asylum, even to see Sam. It was too risky. Mack had just left him there in his recliner that day, saying he was going out to buy supplies. Eventually Sam would figure out he wasn't coming back, and that was okay. Sam was on his own now, and he'd be just fine. After all, he'd been dead since that night they'd escaped thirty years ago.

Lying on the porch in the moonlight next to Ezekiel, Mack thought back to the night he and Sam had escaped from Angola. Sam had bitched and moaned every second during their escape. There was no reason for his concern — Mack had planned everything. He paid off a guard to get him the HVAC layout, and they had gotten away without a hitch. Sam was supposed to be Mack's friend, but Mack knew now he couldn't trust him to keep quiet. He had to go.

The third man who'd escaped with them was Thomas Small. Mack never intended to keep him alive. He had been crazy as a loon, but Mack had to let him come along because he'd threatened to rat Mack out if he didn't. Being right next door, Thomas watched them work on the tunnel, and that night he escaped with Mack and Sam.

They stole a pickup truck, and Mack said he'd drive. Sam got in the middle, and as Thomas was climbing in, Mack came around with a tire iron and crushed his skull. By damn if that didn't make Sam Gold cry! What the hell had that been about, anyway? Mack knew Sam well. Sam was a merciless killer — he'd gunned down all those people at that burger joint — but now they were free, something had snapped in his head. That disappointed Mack very much; Sam was his only friend, but if he didn't get his shit together fast, he was a dead man. If Mack would stay free and alive, there was no place for whimpering pussies who could ruin everything.

Mack headed south to Iberia Parish, far from the prison at Angola and home to a place they could hide out. Mack worked on a plan while Sam sat in the middle, sniveling like a little kid about the dead body touching his arm. Whatever was wrong with Sam, Mack knew what had to be done.

When they were driving along Lake Fausse Pointe, Mack had an amazing stroke of luck. Two guys in their thirties — hobos, from the looks of them — stood on the side of the road next to the lake, thumbs out. Two guys hitchhiking at 3:30 in the morning. It just couldn't get any better than that.

Mack stopped the truck, got out, talked with them long enough to learn they were making their way cross-country from Florida to California, and then he beat them to death with the tire iron. They didn't know what hit them, they were so stoned. Sam witnessed the gory event and became hysterical. Mack stripped down and swapped clothes with one of the dead men. "We'll never get away," Sam kept saying, even when Mack made him get out and help put the bodies into the cab.

"What are you going to do?" Sam asked at last, and Mack showed him. He ran the truck into the lake.

Then Mack picked up the tire iron and guided Sam off down the highway. "Come on, buddy. We're going to the Asylum. We'll be safe there."

Mack took his friend to his secret hiding place — the underground room he'd created for himself as a teenager. Once they got there, Sam was shaking and saying how he would be better off just to turn himself in. But now he'd seen Mack's hideout, and the party was over for him. Mack used the tire iron to put his friend out of his misery.

Even with Sam dead, Mack wanted companionship. He put Sam in the earthen tunnel for six months until he dried out pretty good, and then he positioned the corpse in the recliner so Mack could talk to him whenever he wanted. Sam had sat there for thirty years, and even when Ezekiel came along, Mack still included Sam in the conversations. They'd been friends for a long, long time, after all. Ezekiel told Mack he was crazy, but Mack liked Sam better than Ezekiel, so he told his new friend to shut the hell up.

Then he'd made his one mistake. He should never have locked that kid and his girlfriend up in the Hole. It was a stupid, spur-of-the-moment decision, and now he worried it could bring him down. Somehow those two had escaped, and now the cops had found his secret place.

He snapped out of his reverie and back to the precarious situation at hand. They were on the run now, and it was only a matter of time until the cops figured out where they were.

As he and Ezekiel slowly got up from the porch, he said, "Remember when we kidnapped that guy and his girlfriend? I was just thinking what a mistake that was."

"Yeah," Ezekiel agreed. "You made a huge mistake. That one could cost you."

"It really wasn't my mistake though, was it? I let you take care of feeding them one time and they got away. I should have done it myself. You screwed that up like everything else."

Ezekiel was nervous. He hadn't seen Mack this way — belligerent and mean. Mack never treated him like that. They were friends.

"I was trying to help. I'm not as good as you are at these things."

"That's because I spent time at Angola. I'm hard, Ezekiel, and you're soft."

Someday before long he'd have to take care of this friend too, Mack thought, brushing off a momentary regret and telling himself it was Ezekiel's problem, not his, and he'd handle it when the time came. He'd miss his friend, but now his survival was all that mattered.

The cabin's front door was unlocked, as it always had been when Ezekiel stayed here before. That doctor who owned it apparently had never come back to secure it, and that was a good thing. Maybe they could stay here for a while. Right now they needed rest.

Mack and Ezekiel collapsed into bed at three a.m. and were still sound asleep at daybreak when Sheriff Willie Barbour and a cadre of deputies and state policemen assembled at the Charenton dock where a fisherman's boat had been stolen last night. Teams got into six boats and made ready to cast off. Their mission was to search for Mack Thorn.

The sheriff was certain Thorn had stolen the boat and gone into the bayou. Nobody stole boats around here, especially an old clunker like that one. The river was less than two miles from where the preacher had held his tent revival. Their fugitive was out here somewhere.

Sheriff Barbour's teams headed out around seven, half heading south and half north. They slowly examined the shoreline first on one side, then the other, and checked out every island along the way.

By nine, Mack and Ezekiel were awake and sitting on the front porch. The provisions Ezekiel had brought earlier were still there, and Mack was glad to find coffee. He was beginning to feel himself again, clearheaded and alert after a few hours of much-needed sleep.

"How are you feeling?" he asked Ezekiel, engaging in idle conversation.

"Better. That run took the breath out of me. How'd they find you, Mack? How'd they put us two together? When those cops came in and shouted for you, I looked around. I thought maybe you were standing on the platform behind me, but I didn't see you."

"I don't want to talk about it. Waste of time dwelling on things we can't control. What matters is that we got away. But they'll come. You know they will. And if we stay here, they'll find us."

"They're not after me."

Mack laughed his usual throaty, gravelly laugh. "Oh yeah? They're using you to find me. You're as wanted as I am and you know it."

He'd wanted to ask Ezekiel something for a long time, and now was as good a chance as any.

"You wouldn't ever rat me out, would you, Ezekiel?"

The evangelist had a shocked look on his face. "Are you serious? Why would you think that? You know me better than that."

"We're getting older. Maybe that's why. I thought for a minute last night you might not make it to the bayou. Your heart isn't what it used to be."

"Yours either. Let's be honest, Mack. We're no spring chickens, but what does that have to do with betraying you? I'd never do that!"

Mack's face turned dark. He growled, "No, you wouldn't. Because if I ever thought you might, I'd make your last minutes on earth the most horrible thing you could imagine."

His sudden rage startled Ezekiel. Why was Mack doing this? They were friends. They were inseparable. But Mack was totally unpredictable. This kind of thing scared Ezekiel about him. He was a deranged killer, and Ezekiel knew from experience that Mack had thoughts that were way off base. Sometimes he acted on them, like when he had kidnapped those two people the other night at the Asylum. There was no need for that, even though it was the anniversary. Ezekiel had even asked Mack why he wanted them, but his friend had only smiled that evil smirk.

Ezekiel figured Mack had intended to rape the girl. He hadn't had a woman in a long time, so maybe that was his plan for her. The guy had simply been there too, and presuming Mack didn't have any specific ideas for him, he'd probably have ended up killing them both if the guy hadn't somehow gotten loose. Mack blamed him for that, but it was Mack's fault. They shouldn't have ever taken them. It was too dangerous and look where it had gotten them. Now Mack was on the run for the first time in thirty years, and so was Ezekiel.

"Mack, I swear to you I'd never rat you out. We're a team."

"For as long as I say so. Keep that in mind, my friend. We're a team because I say we are."

Ezekiel shut his mouth. When Mack got this way, it was better to leave things alone. He'd get over it. He always did.

CHAPTER THIRTY-THREE

They sat on the porch for a long time, the stillness of the island broken only by the rustling of tree limbs in a slight breeze and the calls of birds from somewhere in the forest. But then there came another sound — the unmistakable sound of an outboard motor.

"They're coming!" Ezekiel shouted, but Mack was already on his feet. He looked around the cabin, straightened up the room a little, and then they hurried to the boat. Mack started the engine; the cops wouldn't hear it over the din of their own motors. And the lawmen were still a good distance away — maybe a mile or two. They had plenty of time, and he'd already decided where he'd go next. He turned upriver towards Jeanerette, two or three miles away.

"Where are we going?" Ezekiel asked.

"Back to the Asylum. If the cops are all out here looking for us, I figure they've finished at the Asylum. They'd never expect me to go back there."

Ezekiel wasn't so sure. "But what if they haven't left? What if they're still there?"

"Dammit," Mack snarled. "Quit whining, for God's sake! I'm in charge here. You're along for the ride. If I need your advice, I'll ask for it!"

Avoiding the main dock at Jeanerette, he pulled up to a pier that belonged to a housing addition along the bayou. There were parents and kids in their yards, but no one gave Mack a glance. They found the highway and walked toward Victory, staying close to the trees and out of sight of passing cars.

"How far is it?"

Mack sighed. "What if I told you it was five miles? Could you make it if it meant you would stay free?"

"Sure," he answered, already wheezing just a little from the exertion.

"Okay. It's only two. Get your ass in gear and let's get this over with."

As Mack had predicted, there were no cars and no people at the Asylum. Everything was quiet. They walked around the building and back toward the old cemetery where the alternate entrance to Mack's living area was. In the trees where three hundred bodies lay, they came to a spot where Mack cleared leaves away from a four-foot-square metal plate and pulled it open. This was the back entrance to the place he called home.

The trees rustled and whispered.

Come here. Come stay with us, the wind sighed.

"They're talking again," Ezekiel commented. "Can you understand what they're saying?"

"Sure. Do they scare you?" Mack sneered.

"I know what they are just like you do. It doesn't scare me when they talk, but I don't care much for looking at them. And I wish they weren't always calling us to go in there."

"It's a cemetery, for God's sake. You're a grown man. Pull yourself together." Mack gestured to the hole that he'd uncovered. "Go down there and check it out."

"Why me? Why don't you go first?"

"Because the cops are looking for me, that's why."

They're looking for both of us and you know it, Ezekiel thought as he descended the ladder into the room.

Ezekiel said the place was empty, and Mack came in, pulling the plate closed as he descended the ladder.

"Sam's gone," Ezekiel commented, pointing to the recliner, but Mack didn't turn around. He was looking for something. He pulled back a chair, looked at the dirt wall behind it, and cursed.

"Dammit! They took my gun!"

He'd stolen a .38 pistol years ago, put it in a plastic bag, and hid it in a recess in the wall. There had been no need for it until now, but time was drawing short, and Mack knew he had to be ready. Ezekiel was too timid and weak to help now. Soon he'd be gone, and Mack Thorn would be alone once again.

"What do we do now, Mack?"

Mack went to a cabinet, gathered a few things, and put them in a sack. He handed Ezekiel a flashlight. "We're going to visit some old friends. Come along, Ezekiel. Follow me."

Mack led Ezekiel down the earthen corridor that led into the dungeon where he'd chained the couple who got away. He told Ezekiel where to direct the light, and he put three candles from his sack on the massive wooden table that sat in the middle of the room. He struck a match and lit them, and then he said, "Come out, everyone. Come out."

What began as a barely perceptible swishing sound — the sound a broom makes when it's run along a wood floor

217

— became something else. Now it was more like a babbling brook running over stones.

As the sound intensified, Ezekiel whirled about, watching as wispy films of something began to float from the cells that lined the ancient torture chamber. The light from the candles cast an eerie shadow on the vaporous, ethereal strings of smoky haze that were swirling everywhere in the room now. In another setting they might have been beautiful, but here, in this godless room where men were mercilessly beaten and maimed, the things in the air were ghostly, evil parts of the past.

The sound grew louder and louder, a crescendo of noise that became a cacophony of words — a screaming chaos of discord. There were a hundred wisps of vapor in the air now, spinning crazily around the table where Mack and Ezekiel stood.

HELP ME!

KILL ME PLEASE! LET ME GO!!

DON'T. PLEASE DON'T.

And then the laughing began — the cruel, merciless, heartless cackles of depraved guards who tortured the prisoners for pleasure. The laughing was like the other sounds at first — low and swishy and distant, then louder and louder until the screaming sniggers of crazed men no better than their captives filled the room completely.

Mack looked at Ezekiel and began to laugh. The flickering candles blazed in his eyes like fire, and he roared, "Are you enjoying this? These are my people, Ezekiel. All of them — guards and inmates alike. They're psychos just like me, without a soul or conscience, enjoying what they can do to hurt other people. This is my world!"

Ezekiel shrank back in horror. Mack wasn't surprised at what was going on right now. Obviously he'd engaged in this ritual before. How could Ezekiel have missed the signs that this man was completely, totally insane?

For the first time since he'd known Mack, he was terrified of him. Watching him wave his arms in the air like a symphony's director, Ezekiel knew beyond a doubt that before it was over, this crazed individual would kill him.

He had to figure out how to stop all this, now. Mack was close to entering a place from which he might never return. And he was willing to go there.

Ezekiel swooped his hands around and extinguished the candles.

CHAPTER THIRTY-FOUR

"What are you doing?" As the candles went out, Mack's maniacal scream was that of a madman, a psychotic thing that had lost its mind.

Ezekiel directed the flashlight around. The wispy things in the air had disappeared, and except for Mack's ranting, the room was completely quiet.

"You must stop this insanity. It's not right."

Mack's face transformed from a twisted grimace into calmness. The fire in his eyes was gone, and his snarl was a half-smile. It was a disturbing metamorphosis that reminded Ezekiel of Dr. Jekyll.

"What were you doing, Mack?" Ezekiel said. He had to keep it together in order to stop Mack from going back to where he'd just been. "What was that all about, anyway?"

"They're coming for me. And I'm going with them. I won't let them take me again. No more cells for me. I'm going with my friends."

"What friends? I'm your only friend."

Mack laughed easily this time, not the cackle of a madman but the easy chuckle of someone who'd heard a funny joke. "Oh, Ezekiel. How little you understand. My friends are here. I'm going with them."

At last Ezekiel got it. Mack was talking about the wispy things he'd conjured up a moment ago. He called them his friends — the prisoners from the Asylum from more than a hundred years ago. The ones who beckoned to him from the cemetery. The ones who were in this chamber and in the main building. The ones who'd died horrific deaths at the hands of brutal guards.

Mack's people.

Ezekiel didn't know what was up Mack's sleeve. "What's next?"

Ezekiel saw the look of resignation on Mack's face. They were both too old to stay on the run anymore. Mack had ruined the secret life that had kept him free, and he'd ruined Ezekiel's life too. The only thing left for them was to die in prison…or to escape. The permanent kind of escape. That was what Mack was talking about.

Mack said, "I want to go to the Asylum one last time. Up to the top. I owe it to them."

Ezekiel understood. In the massive building that had caged all those lost, hopeless souls, Mack would perform this bizarre ritual one more time. He wanted to commune with his friends, the ones that occupied the hell he would soon visit himself. Maybe today would be the day Mack would go away. Ezekiel understood why it had to happen, and this time he led the way for his friend Mack.

They went up into the old kitchen, opened the door, and stepped outside into the sunshine. Two old friends walked across the broad lawn to the main building.

Landry perked up when he saw someone in the yard. He'd been expecting to see Mack Thorn go into the kitchen building, but he came out instead. He wasn't sure it was Mack because he was too far away to see a face. He snapped a few pictures, but he didn't have enough details to call the police just yet. Carefully, cautiously, he followed. He didn't intend to be captured again.

The old structure creaked and groaned like always as Ezekiel and Mack climbed the stairs to the fourth floor. In the hallway that lined the cellblock, Ezekiel stood to one side as Mack took more candles from his sack, lit one, dripped wax on the floor, and stuck all three upright. He lit the other two, stood and began to chant.

"Come out. Come out, everyone. Come join me."

This time it was vastly different. Instead of an underground chamber filled with wispy things, there were hundreds and hundreds that floated from empty cells, up the metal stairways and through the windows. It seemed that many trapped spirits of doomed men inhabited this dark, dismal place, and they were all answering Mack's invitation.

Now the noises came again, louder and louder until they were deafening screams from a choir of ghostly voices. The apparitions were every bit as terrifying as before, but Ezekiel was more prepared. He felt they wouldn't harm him. They wanted recognition, and Mack was giving it to them. He was a kindred soul — another doomed, insane criminal just like they were. But he was alive, and he gave them the freedom to speak.

As he crept up the stairs, Landry hit one creaking metal riser after another. He paused each time he made a noise, but as he got higher, he heard sounds from above, as though someone were hosting a party for a hundred guests, all of whom were mingling and conversing at once. Whoever was up there wouldn't be able to hear him. He kept going.

He gripped his phone. He'd prepared a text message for Lieutenant Kanter earlier, telling him where Landry was and that he'd found Mack Thorn. All he had to do was press a button to send the text, and the detective would come find him. Cate would get it too; she was a part of this and deserved to know.

He carefully ascended the stairs to the fourth floor, and he stuck his head up into the room far enough to see. He couldn't believe what was happening; he switched to video and started recording the unearthly scene playing out in the hallway.

The light from three candles on the floor illuminated a cloud of vaporous wisps — things Landry somehow knew were men's souls — who moaned, screamed, cried, wailed and danced around the candles. The ghostly apparitions whirled around the candles in tighter and tighter circles. Someone was inside the ring that they were spinning around, but there were so many dense clouds of screaming souls that Landry couldn't make out who was there. He pressed the button and sent his text.

Ezekiel and Mack stood back to back inside the three candles, unable to move as the things whirled around them, pressing on their arms and making it difficult to draw a breath.

"It's over," Mack said in a raspy whisper Ezekiel could barely hear. "Put out the candles and let them rest."

But Ezekiel couldn't reach the candles. He couldn't bend down and neither could Mack. The things he had unleashed were holding them prisoner.

Mack kicked at a candle and it tipped over, rolling somewhere. Ezekiel stomped at another and then gave a wild kick and knocked away the third.

As before, the ethereal wisps disappeared in an instant, and the room was silent.

Without a word between them, Mack led the way downstairs to their next stop. Ezekiel knew where it was. It was the last place Mack would go to see his friends.

From one of the empty cells on the third floor, Landry watched everything. He saw the candle kicked away and heard the noises that suddenly stopped. He'd scurried down the stairs to get out of sight, heedless of whatever noise he was making but hopeful whatever was going on upstairs would preoccupy the killer he'd unmasked.

Mack and Ezekiel walked out the back of the building, past the kitchen and into the trees that marked the cemetery. Landry followed at a healthy distance, keeping out of sight.

Up on the fourth floor of the Asylum, one solitary candle — the one Mack had kicked away — lay in a corner.

It was still burning brightly.

CHAPTER THIRTY-FIVE

It wouldn't take candles or a ritual this time, Ezekiel realized as they walked into the graveyard. This was where these lost souls lived. This was their place of damnation — their home, if such a godforsaken plot of ground could be called a home. This was where three hundred dead men were trapped in a purgatory with no hope and no peace.

There was some unseen signal between the things that lived here and the ones Mack had conjured up in the dungeon and the building. These ghostly wisps were already busy, spinning wildly above plots of earth with wooden crosses — their markers, the only thing that identified them as human beings. While they lived, they had never been treated as human, but now Mack was calling them together in a conclave of the damned.

They spoke to him.

Come, brother!

Come to us. Join us here.

Come and be one with us!

Ezekiel stepped aside as Mack strode confidently to the middle of the cemetery. He watched — as did Landry — while the wispy tendrils caressed Mack's face and arms. The sounds grew louder and more concentrated. Their voices were different from before — they were one voice now, one singular, commanding voice — and they told Mack what to do.

Sit here, brother.

Sit here on this stone. Take out your knife. Open it.

Things were getting out of hand, Ezekiel thought with growing alarm. Mack sat down on a large rock amid the graves, pulled a switchblade from his pocket and opened it. Ezekiel could hear sirens, but he was mesmerized by the scene before him. He knew he should run, but he had to see this one to the end. It was time for it to be over.

The things that whirled around Mack were quieter now. They were whispering to him, and he was smiling and answering as if he was talking to a friend. Mack spoke easily as he tested the sharpness of the blade with his finger.

Tinkling, almost musical sounds came from the wispy clouds. *Welcome, Mack. We hoped you'd join us.*

Mack's answer was rough and gravelly, as always. "I've known you were here since I first came to the Asylum."

Whispers, soft and breezy. *Be one with us. Use the knife.*

"I'm not sure I want to do it. Are you in Hell?"

We're right here. Come and join us.

As Landry watched this incredibly bizarre scene from the other side of the cemetery, watching a man talking to a swirling mass of tendrils, he texted Kanter his location. The sirens were much louder; he knew it wouldn't be long.

Suddenly the wispy images came together as one and flew upwards. They descended upon Landry, winding tightly around him until he couldn't move. Mack's eyes widened in surprise as he watched the wisps pull and tug Landry, pushing him down next to Mack on the rock.

Kill him!

Plunge your knife into his heart!

Kill him, brother! NOW!

"No, Mack! Stop it!" Ezekiel shouted as Kanter and three uniformed cops burst into the grove of trees.

The ethereal clouds rose again and swirled around the cops, who were enveloped by the angry, whirling things. They created a barrier; the officers could see what was happening, but when they pushed forward, a pulsating wall held them back, and hundreds of voices whispered, *"No! No! No!"*

Ezekiel ran to Mack, jerked the knife from his hand and screamed, "Mack, this has to stop. Now!"

"Ezekiel, don't do it! I'm not ready!" Mack cried as his friend drove the blade into Mack's chest, burying it to the hilt.

At that very second, the swirling things disappeared and it was quiet. All that was left now was the rustling of tree limbs. Lieutenant Kanter ran to Landry, who sat immobile by the body of Mack Thorn that lay on the ground beside him.

"Are you okay?" he shouted, and Landry nodded. The detective took Mack's pulse and shook his head.

Kanter turned to Landry. "I could barely hear what he said. Did he say 'Mack, this has to stop, now' right before he killed himself?"

Landry nodded. He was groggy and disoriented. Until a moment ago, he was certain that he was going to die himself. "He stuck that knife into his own chest. My God, did you see that? And he talked to himself. He called himself Mack, but this isn't Mack Thorn. This is a preacher named Ezekiel

Billings. I've seen him before. What's going on, Lieutenant? What the hell just happened?"

As he and the detective talked, Landry looked past him and broke into a faint smile. Cate was running toward him. Something inside him stirred with emotions as she hugged him tightly.

She recoiled at the body on the ground beside him, and Lieutenant Kanter helped Landry up, guiding them both away from the cemetery and giving them a little time to themselves.

"Thank you for coming," he said weakly. "This has all been so bizarre."

"I can't imagine what you've been through. I feel responsible. I'm the one who brought you here in the first place."

"Thanks, but don't forget I'm the one who trespassed here twice before I ever met you. This isn't your fault. It isn't mine either. We just got caught up in something..." He paused. "Cate, you know there are supernatural things going on here. We heard sounds when Mack had us chained up. They're ghosts."

She raised her eyebrows slightly. She wanted to believe him, but with what he'd just witnessed, she wasn't sure how clearly he was thinking.

"I saw the spirits of the dead prisoners. Ask Lieutenant Kanter — he saw them too. They were talking to Mack, urging him to kill himself and join them. He had a battle going on within himself. Ezekiel was telling him to stop while Mack wanted to get it over with. In the end, Mack won."

"All I care about is that you're safe." She hugged him again, and he put his arms around her, pulling her close to him and thinking how wonderful it felt that she cared.

Just then there were shouts from the cops. They turned and saw flames shooting from the windows on the Asylum's top floor. Thick black smoke billowed upwards into the approaching night. Lieutenant Kanter called for help, but they all knew the building was doomed. The nearest fire department was fifteen miles away. Jeanerette's volunteer fire brigade was closer, but it had only two pumper units, no match for an old wooden building. Kanter ushered everyone out of the cemetery, leaving one cop to guard it, and secured the sides of the burning building to keep people away from the crime scene behind it.

Sheriff's deputies arrived at the same time as the Jeanerette firemen. Ten minutes later, six units from the New Iberia Fire Department arrived, followed shortly after by a helicopter carrying a news crew from New Orleans.

It took a DNA match and a lesson in psychiatry before the mystery of what happened at the Asylum was solved. The dead man really was Mack Thorn. The crazed individual sitting on the rock in the cemetery — the man that Cate's father had kicked off the island — was the man who escaped from Angola in 1988.

Landry and the cops had seen Mack talk to himself. He called himself by name, told himself this all had to stop, and he had screamed that he wasn't ready to die. He had yelled "Ezekiel, no!" to someone else — but no one else was there. There was no Ezekiel Billings except in the dark corners of Mack Thorn's mind. The moment that Mack plunged the switchblade deep into his own chest, the only other living people in the cemetery were Landry and the cops.

There had been no one else. Nobody walked across the grass but Mack. Nobody performed the ritual on the fourth floor except Mack. Nobody spoke to ghostly apparitions in the cemetery but Mack.

Psychiatrists speculated that long ago, when Mack invented the evangelist and started preaching, Ezekiel had been a character he could slip into and out of. But Ezekiel had become something else — a completely different person. The two of them engaged in conversation, told stories and went on adventures together. They were two separate individuals, the experts explained, even though Ezekiel existed only inside Mack's twisted mind.

The psychiatrist's report described a bizarre situation. Mack suffered from a rare form of schizophrenia wherein Billings, his alter ego or secondary personality, actually was a unique person. When Ezekiel was in control, he was completely different. His thoughts, memories, dreams and realities were his only. His personality differed from Mack's — Ezekiel had a conscience, for instance — but like Mack he was a disturbed, troubled man, haunted by carnal desires and false declarations of faith. He had been revered as a man of the cloth, but it was simply a charade to make a living and get out of that dank underground room where Mack lived. He had saved souls, but he always wondered if he had condemned those new Christians to damnation, since he didn't believe himself. When those sins tore deeply enough into Ezekiel's conscience, he had simply retreated and let Mack take over.

Unlike Mack, Billings didn't have a violent, brutal streak. There had never been a claim of impropriety against the evangelist in more than a decade of preaching in rural towns and spending the night in one home after another. If the people who welcomed the congenial evangelist into their homes and their lives had known that an insane rapist and murderer lived somewhere inside the affable preacher's mind, they would have been horrified. But it remained a secret, all the way to the grave.

Of course people wondered what happened to Reverend Billings. Those who were at the tent revival that night would recall that the police were looking for someone else. So why did the preacher run away? Maybe he had a past. Maybe he wasn't what people thought he was.

Some people did internet searches. They found reports about the successful revivals he'd conducted around this part of Louisiana in the past three years. But that was it — there was no biography, no credentials from some seminary where he got his divinity degree, no past at all. He'd just started evangelizing one night, or so it appeared. He'd been loved by many, sought after by tiny churches, and hailed for his mighty oration, but who he actually was remained a mystery, because Ezekiel Billings was never heard from again.

CHAPTER THIRTY-SIX

Sunday night, a week after the fire

Thousands of viewers tuned in for Channel Nine's much-anticipated special report, "Victory and the House of Horrors." Seven days after the fire, the ruins of the huge old building still smoldered, and one pumper truck stayed on scene to control hot spots.

The program began with five pictures that covered two hundred years of history — a magnificent hotel, a cadre of Union troops standing outside their temporary barracks, a penitentiary, an eerie, abandoned building, and now a pile of smoky debris.

A newscaster in her twenties introduced Henri Duchamp, a scholarly-looking man with a goatee, horn-rimmed glasses and a bow tie who was president of the Louisiana Society for the Paranormal. He explained that when gruesome things happen inside a building, powerful, negative energy is released, often spawning extrasensory or paranormal events.

The spirits of those who died — their souls, some people say — cannot break free from the terror they experienced. Because they are still there, sounds, visions and movements occur. That's why it's appropriate to call it a "haunted" place.

He explained that when one or two bad things happen in a house or a building — a mass murder, for example — spirits may manifest themselves to some people, but others won't observe anything. But in the case of the Asylum, where hundreds upon hundreds of prisoners suffered terrifying horrors, the place was bursting with negative energy. He explained that was why everybody who went into that building experienced the spirit manifestations. The ghosts of the dead were doomed to inhabit the place where they were persecuted.

Duchamp added, "There's no other building in Louisiana — maybe not anywhere on earth — where so many ghastly things happened to so many people. That's why it's undoubtedly the most haunted building in our state."

"Let's roll the video," the newscaster said, and viewers watched footage shot by people who went to the Asylum over several years. Since the interior was perpetually gloomy, the images were fuzzy and unclear, but Duchamp explained what each one represented, even if the public might not see it the way he did. Where viewers saw wispy, filmy clouds, the expert called them spirits of people — a man here, two more over there. And here's one wrapped in chains, he said, pointing to another translucent substance floating in the air.

There were sounds too — scratchy recordings that might have been a wail, or a voice saying "help me" or "I'm dying" — but those watching the show needed a good deal of imagination to agree that those sounds came from the undead.

The newscaster spoke now, saying the "most haunted" nickname was even more fitting now. Landry Drake, who works for the *Daily Iberian* newspaper, connected many years of mysterious deaths on the same day — June 10. In 2012 three college students, sent into the building on a fraternity pledge prank, were gruesomely murdered.

The latest deaths occurred in June of last year when two bodies were discovered, one in the old prison cemetery and another in the house. State police called it a drug-related murder and suicide, although the medical examiner's conclusion they died on June 10 caught Landry's attention, and he added those names to his growing list.

Landry's interview came next, followed by the video he'd shot on the top floor of the Asylum as Mack Thorn carried out his uncanny ritual. Unlike the footage shown earlier in the broadcast, Landry's recording was riveting. The translucent things that whirled around and around Mack Thorn were impossible to miss seeing, and their plaintive wails and moans were chilling.

He described his and Cate's kidnapping and how they escaped. He went back, he said, and witnessed the eerie ritual performed by Mack Thorn and his alternate personality, Ezekiel Billings. It was a spellbinding account guaranteed to keep viewers tuned in, and the high ratings proved they were captivated by this subject.

"Regardless of your opinion about ghosts," the newscaster concluded, "one thing is certain. Inmates at the Asylum endured unspeakable horrors for many years. Hundreds died there, and unexplainable things have happened since it closed in 1907. Many people have seen ghostly lights in the windows, and don't forget the hundreds of bodies buried in the cemetery near Bayou Teche. People boating on the bayou often report hearing eerie sounds coming from that area. Even stranger are the unexplained deaths over the past thirty years that make it clear why our guest Henri Duchamp calls the Asylum 'most haunted.' We can hope that the fire that destroyed the two-hundred-year-old building will allow the spirits to be free at last. For that, we must wait and see. Thanks for watching and have a good evening."

CHAPTER THIRTY-SEVEN

Six Months Later
The French Quarter, New Orleans

Cate sat in a chair twenty feet from Landry, in the shadows while he was under hot, bright lights. During every break, a makeup artist dabbed his face with a tissue and applied powder where droplets of sweat had formed.

Tonight was the first time he'd invited her to watch the crew taping a show. For four hours, she had seen takes and retakes that would become ninety minutes of footage, and two hours with commercials. Landry and a news anchor sat behind a desk emblazoned with a network logo. A man raised his hand, counted down from five to one, and lowered it. Cate's heart raced as she watched the anchor begin the show.

Good evening. I'm Ken Spearman and tonight Channel Nine's investigative reporter, Landry Drake, is joining me for a very interesting story. His face has become familiar over the past several months, not only here in Louisiana but across the country. Landry told his incredible firsthand account of a weekend of terror at the Victory Institution for the Criminally Insane — better known as the Asylum — in Iberia Parish.

This is another of our Forgotten Men *documentaries — a story of prisoners who endured unspeakable horrors at the Asylum. In previous segments, we have walked with Landry through the most haunted building in Louisiana. He showed us its glory days as the Hotel Iberia, once the grandest hotel in the South. We followed its transition from hotel to Union army barracks to prison. We walked through the underground chamber where inmates were tortured and killed, and we heard a chilling story of how he spent one terrifying weekend as a prisoner himself.*

Tonight's segment — "The Escape" — reveals how a deranged killer serving a life sentence at Angola Prison broke out, came back to his home parish, killed and killed again without being caught for thirty years.

I'll remind our viewers that this series contains graphic material that may make you uneasy. It's not a show for young children, but it's a story that must be told.

And now it's my pleasure to introduce Landry Drake, who'll give us the story of Mad Mack Thorn's escape and disappearance for thirty years.

Even though Landry couldn't see her because of the lights, she gave him a huge smile and a wave. It excited her to be in the studio, and Landry's success made her proud of him. He had hoped someday to use his journalism degree, and thanks to their awful experience, he was both using it and famous too.

Good evening, everyone. I'm Landry Drake, Channel Nine's investigative reporter. Thanks for joining us. As Ken said, tonight you'll hear another bizarre, true story in our

FORGOTTEN MEN: THE BAYOU HAUNTINGS

Forgotten Men series *about a long-abandoned prison, a ghost town in Iberia Parish and an escaped convict who eluded the law for thirty years.*

Most reporters aren't part of the stories they tell. They present the facts as they understand them, they try to imagine the feelings of the participants, they paint a picture of what happened, and they weave a tale they hope is close to reality. This story is different because everything you'll see tonight is true, and I was part of it.

This incredible tale begins thirty years ago, on a winter night back in 1988 when three men escaped from the maximum-security Louisiana State Penitentiary at Angola. The convicts had things in common. All from Iberia Parish, each was serving a long sentence for brutal, violent crimes. Since they grew up in the same parish, officials assumed they'd been friends before prison, but that wasn't true.

Mackey Thorn, a deranged individual nicknamed "Mad Mack" since elementary school, was convicted in 1977 for the ax murder of a teenaged girl. They found her body in a remote area along the banks of the Bayou Teche. The other escapees were Samuel Gold, a mass murderer sent to Angola in 1979, and Thomas Small, a rapist who entered prison in 1980.

The men lived in the same cellblock at Angola. Thorn and Gold were cellmates at the time of the escape, and Thomas Small was next door. For weeks, they dug a tunnel, entering through a wall behind a toilet. The warden called it an inside job because the convicts knew where to go, but that was never proven. The three entered a vast system of air ducts, crawled up a narrow ventilation pipe and popped out onto the roof of the administration building, outside the massive concrete walls and razor-wire fences. Then they climbed down a fire escape and disappeared.

241

Angola penitentiary is up on the Mississippi border, a hundred and twenty miles north of New Iberia. Today it's home to the state's most violent and incorrigible offenders, but it hasn't always been that way. From 1875 until 1907, prisoners the state classified as criminally insane ended up at the Asylum in Victory.

Not everyone sent to Victory was mentally ill. The Asylum became a dumping ground for the state's problems. One of America's first private prisons, it became the place where the state handed over their worst to someone else.

I spent a terrifying sixty minutes in the Asylum as a teenager because I accepted a dare. I made fifty bucks from my brother that afternoon for spending an hour in the abandoned building, but twelve years later I still shudder when I recall the feeling that evil permeated every inch of the place. Later, I experienced that evil firsthand when my friend and I were chained to a wall in a dungeon underground for two days. We've covered that story in a previous segment, so let's get back to the escape.

The inmates were discovered missing after a four a.m. bed check, and the state police searched every house within a five-mile radius of the prison. They knocked on doors, rousting people from their beds, and one man who lived just a mile from Angola gave the cops their first clue. Someone had stolen a truck from his front yard. He admitted he'd left the keys in it like many folks did, and he'd heard nothing unusual, but his truck had disappeared.

A year later authorities believed they'd solved the mystery of the escaped convicts. During an unusually dry summer, two fishermen on Lake Fausse Pointe saw the tailgate of a pickup sticking out of the water a few feet from shore. It hadn't been visible until the water level was down. When the cops pulled it out, they looked in the cab and learned what had happened to the escapees. They had come back home to Iberia Parish. Three bodies were in such a state of advanced decomposition that identification was impossible, but there were plenty of clues. There was the stolen truck from Angola, with three bodies inside, two still wearing their orange prison shirts and pants. They were males and about the same age, height and build as the escapees.

Authorities closed the case a few days after the truck was discovered. The theory was that somehow they made a wrong turn onto a closed road, drove off into the lake and drowned. That brought a sigh of relief to the people of Iberia Parish, who were at last free from worrying about locking their doors and keeping their kids inside after dark.

When he went off to prison, Mad Mack left behind a wife named Susanna. She was a meek, simple woman who became pregnant at eighteen, married him, and delivered a stillborn girl. Her parents always believed Mack had beaten her that night. Whether that was true, Susanna put up with a lot during her tumultuous marriage to a sadistic criminal. The first ray of sunshine in her pathetic life came when he received a life sentence.

A week after he left, she and Mack's lawyer began seeing each other, and she told her parents she understood for the first time what a real relationship should be. She was happy, free, and she was involved with someone who cared for her. The attorney, James Romero, told friends he found her a refreshing change from the society girls he'd known at Tulane. She was unsophisticated, but instead of being off-putting to him, that innocence made her desirable. From the moment they began dating, the two opposites felt a common attraction too strong to ignore. It wasn't long until she moved in with her boyfriend, and in 1978, a year after Mack left, she filed for divorce. Two days after the divorce was official, she and the prominent attorney married in a quiet civil ceremony.

When Mack escaped in 1988, his ex-wife was concerned that he might come after her. She and her husband spoke to one of the state police investigators, and once they learned the police had no clue as to his whereabouts, the couple became even more concerned. Although Thorn had disappeared, the authorities assured her he'd turn up, because almost everyone did. There was no more information for almost a year.

When they found the bodies, she stopped living in fear at last. From that day forward, her life was filled with happy days and a good marriage — until the night of June 10, 1991. The next morning, her husband failed to appear in court for a hearing, and police went to his house. They found a grisly scene. The naked, decapitated bodies of Mad Mack's wife, Susanna, and his lawyer were lying in their bed. In the gory carnage, authorities found the murder weapon, a bloodstained hatchet.

The newspaper reported something everyone in town remembered — an ax murder was what got Mack Thorn sent to Angola for life. Now his ex-wife and her husband — Mack's former lawyer — were dead. Even though the bodies of Mack and his accomplices had been found two years back, people wondered if he could still be alive. They conjured up ghost stories that put goosebumps on the arms of kids and adults alike.

Authorities believed Mack Thorn drowned in that stolen pickup; there was nothing to show otherwise. Without leads on the murder of the prominent lawyer and his wife, the case was put aside, remaining unsolved for more than twenty years.

With good reason, people in New Iberia were frightened once again. There had never been a double murder, and these killings were horrific. The authorities said Mack had died, but the sensational press — the outlets that titillated the senses with fear and dread — conjured up stories of a ghostly murderer walking the rural roads of the parish at night, carrying a bloody hatchet and peeking through bedroom windows to find his next victim. If that didn't make you double-check your locks at night, nothing would. Sales of guns skyrocketed, and pizza deliveries and movie ticket sales plummeted as citizens barricaded themselves in their homes after dark, afraid to open the door for anyone.

Time dulls the memories, and as winter turned to spring, then to summer and fall, things returned to normal in Iberia Parish. Parents still conjured up the ghost of Mad Mack as a tool to corral kids who wanted to stay out after curfew or sleep with their bedroom windows open, but things became calm at last.

With half of the show taped, everyone took a thirty-minute break. Cate told Landry how much she enjoyed the behind-the-scenes look at a broadcast, and that he was doing a great job.

When the second half began, Landry narrated a ten-minute video of Mack's underground lair. He explained that after crime scene investigators left, a single film crew was allowed in to shoot footage that the other networks shared. WVUE Channel 8 had created the video, but tonight's viewers — on Channel Nine — listened to Landry's voice instead of the audio on the tape. His personal knowledge made the description chilling, intense and believable.

Landry pointed out the recliner where Sam Gold's body had sat since 1988, the narrow tunnel that ran from the dungeon, and another one that led to a porthole and up into the yard.

At the end, Landry thanked viewers again for their interest and turned things back to his colleague, who previewed the next installment.

Don't miss our next exciting segment in Forgotten Men, *as Landry takes us into the twisted mind of Mack Thorn, who posed as a traveling evangelist for several years. Unsuspecting members of rural churches across southern Louisiana allowed the Reverend Ezekiel Billings into their homes. They fixed him dinner, introduced him to their children, and allowed him to spend the night in their guest bedrooms. No one realized the friendly, good-natured preacher was a sadistic psychopath.*

This is an incredible segment you must see, one of the strangest chapters in the bizarre story of Mack Thorn and the Asylum. I hope you've enjoyed tonight's show. For now, I'm Ken Spearman. My colleague Landry Drake and I wish you a good evening.

CHAPTER THIRTY-EIGHT

Landry and Cate sipped Sazeracs at the Carousel Bar of the Monteleone Hotel. Their seats rotated around the bar itself, but they were oblivious to everything and everyone in the room. This was their time. Now that Landry's life was a whirlwind of activity, they savored every stolen moment together.

It was a quarter after eleven, and she and Landry had just come from his recording session at the TV station a few blocks away. She raised her glass. "Congratulations on the taping tonight. You did a great job!"

He tapped his against it and said, "The best part of my life is finding you."

A great deal had happened since the night of the fire. Ty Jones, the *Daily Iberian* editor, had fired him when he asked for time off, but once he learned about Landry's stakeout and discovery at the Asylum, he asked if he'd finish the short-term job. Landry had promised not to leave him without a copy editor, so he returned. Now that he was back, he had an outstanding commitment — an article about the Bayou Teche treasure that would require a lot of research.

Lieutenant Kanter called with some great news. For the past thirty years, there had been a ten-thousand-dollar reward for information leading to Mackey Thorn's capture. Kanter had learned about it, and he'd already started the wheels turning. Landry could expect a check within sixty days. That was good news for sure; now he could live on his credit cards until the money arrived.

In the days after the fire, Landry had several interesting offers. Agents called and suggested publicity tours and that he write a book. Three regional TV stations teased him with a broadcasting job.

The actual copy editor at the newspaper — the lady on maternity leave — called Ty Jones to say she wasn't coming back. She loved being a stay-at-home mom, and she wanted to try it for a year.

Facing many interesting possibilities for the future, Landry turned down the full-time position. The editor promoted someone in-house, and ten days later Landry's temporary employment was over.

He agreed to finish the treasure story as an independent stringer. His deadline was nine months away; there was a lot of research to do. His investigative reporting skills honed, he'd finish the article on time and reveal yet another surprise — two vast hoards of pirate treasure had been found by Frank Connolly in the early 1800s. Was more there? It was up to future treasure hunters to find out.

After he left the *Daily Iberian*, Landry took two weeks off, considered his possibilities, got a lot of free advice, and decided what was next in his life. He drove to New Orleans and interviewed for what he considered his most interesting offer. The position they suggested was just what he wanted.

Channel Nine's station manager took a risk hiring a man with no broadcast journalism experience to be its first-ever investigative reporter. Landry Drake's involvement in the strange occurrences at the Asylum convinced him that Landry deserved a shot. His sincere personality, smooth Southern drawl and handsome face made him recognizable and likable to a growing group of fans who considered him a leading authority on the paranormal.

The station manager's gamble turned out well. In the six months since the fire, Landry had been busy. Besides his work at the station, he appeared on several national newscasts and wrote a series that was syndicated to metropolitan dailies across the country. Magazine articles appeared regularly in publications as diverse as the *National Enquirer*, *Parade* and *Reader's Digest*.

Through his recently hired publicist, Landry announced a book would be released in the fall by a major publishing house. The book deal included a six-figure advance, and thanks to a massive publicity campaign, it looked to become a best seller.

One local tour company got the jump on its competitors by locking up rights to visit the old prison. They hired Landry as a consultant, and now busses left New Orleans for a trip to two historic plantation homes on the Mississippi River and a visit to Victory. Along the route, Landry's recorded voice told the tourists what to expect.

The main building lay in ruins, and visitors saw where the grand hotel once stood. They toured the old kitchen, walked down the hidden stairway and entered the dungeon. They saw the cemetery and the crosses, but nothing strange happened. There were no apparitions or ghostly sounds. Perhaps the fire had set the forgotten men free at last, the tour guides recited as part of their spiel.

Channel Nine also loaned Landry to its national network. Between trips to New York for TV appearances and a packed speaking schedule, he was out of town almost all the time these days, and his employer enjoyed the attention the station got as part of Landry's fame. He and Cate were together less often, but when they could squeeze in time together — even at eleven p.m. in a hotel bar — they seized the chance to be alone.

One side effect of fame was a loss of privacy, and tonight was no exception. Four times in thirty minutes, people had interrupted to ask for his autograph and tell Landry about their visits to the site.

"Did all that really happen?" they'd ask. "Being kidnapped and all, weren't you terrified?" "Do you truly believe you saw ghosts?"

He was polite, but he brushed off questions, explaining that he wasn't free to talk now. They'd return to their seats, but Cate saw others point and whisper as they recognized her celebrity boyfriend.

She took his hand. "You're leaving tomorrow for New York again, right?"

"Yes. I'll be gone a couple of days. You're going back home tomorrow, right? If the times work out, we can ride out to the airport together."

After three glorious days here in New Orleans with Landry, she was headed back to Galveston. She checked the flight information on her phone, compared the departure time to his, and agreed she'd go with him.

With a sly look on his face, he said, "Look at your calendar for the weekend after next. There's a place I'd like to see, and I want to take you with me."

Her calendar showed the dates were wide open, and she asked him where they were going.

"I'm taking you to a place called Beau Rivage. I saw it online and read about its history. It's a haunted mansion on the Atchafalaya River a couple of hours from here. A woman named Callie Pilantro owns it; she turned an old antebellum mansion into a bed and breakfast. It's only been open a few months. The pictures on its website look great, the reviews are all five star, and it's got a great spooky history. I thought we could run up there for the weekend, and maybe the owner will give us a tour."

"I know why you want to go. It's right down your alley, ghost hunter. It also sounds like a place Dad would like."

"It does, except that Dad's not invited. This will be a trip just for Cate and Landry."

"I'm in. Book it."

"Leave it to me. Shall I get two rooms, like the last time?"

"I think we know each other a little better now than we did then. Let's save a little of your hard-earned money and book one room."

"Even better. I can read you bedtime stories until you fall asleep."

She laughed and gave him a little kiss. "Bedtime stories work, but I had other ideas."

Just then, an older man in a Hawaiian shirt and shorts stuck his ample frame in between the couple to get Landry's sixth autograph of the evening. Landry asked for his check. He'd always loved the charm of the Carousel Bar. He and Cate had spent some wonderful hours here, but this was too much. He was too well-known now.

"I know a quiet little place we can go for a nightcap," he said as they walked through the hotel's lobby and out onto Royal Street. "It's not as nice as this one, but it's a hell of a lot more private."

"If it's called Landry's Place, I'm in." She grinned, taking his arm as they walked down the sidewalk deeper into the Quarter.

MAY WE OFFER YOU A FREE BOOK?

Bill Thompson's award-winning first novel, *The Bethlehem Scroll*, can be yours free.

Simply go to
billthompsonbooks.com
and click "Subscribe."

Once you're on the list, you'll receive advance notice of future book releases and other offers.

Thank you!

Thanks for reading *Forgotten Men*. I hope you enjoyed the book and I'd really appreciate a review on Amazon, Goodreads or both.
Even a line or two makes a tremendous difference so thanks in advance for your help!

Sincerely, Bill Thompson

Please join me on:
Facebook
http://on.fb.me/187NRRP
Twitter
@BThompsonBooks

Made in the USA
Middletown, DE
21 December 2020